ALEXANDER PUSHKIN

Boris Godunov,
Little Tragedies,
and Others

Alexander Pushkin (1799–1837) was a poet, play-wright, and novelist who achieved literary fame before he was twenty. He was born into the Russian nobil-ity, and his great-grandfather was the African-born general Abram Petrovich Gannibal. Pushkin's radical politics brought him censorship and periods of banish-ment, but he eventually married a society beauty and became part of court life. Notoriously touchy about his honor, he died at age thirty-seven in a duel with his wife's alleged lover.

Richard Pevear and Larissa Volokhonsky have trans-lated works by Tolstoy, Dostoevsky, Chekhov, Gogol, Bulgakov, Leskov, and Pasternak. They have been twice awarded the PEN/Book-of-the-Month Club Transla-tion Prize (for Dostoevsky's *The Brothers Karamazov* and Tolstoy's *Anna Karenina*), and their translation of Dostoevsky's *Demons* was one of three nominees for the same prize. They are married and live in France.

Boris Godunov,
Little Tragedies,
and Others

Boris Godunov, Little Tragedies, and Others

THE COMPLETE PLAYS

Alexander Pushkin

Translated from the Russian by
Richard Pevear and Larissa Volokhonsky

Vintage Classics
VINTAGE BOOKS
A DIVISION OF PENGUIN RANDOM HOUSE LLC
NEW YORK

A VINTAGE CLASSICS ORIGINAL 2023

English-language translation copyright © 2023
by Richard Pevear and Larissa Volokhonsky
Introduction copyright © 2023 by Richard Pevear

All rights reserved. Published in the United States
by Vintage Books, a division of Penguin Random House LLC,
New York, and distributed in Canada by
Penguin Random House Canada Limited, Toronto.

Vintage is a registered trademark
and Vintage Classics and colophon are trademarks
of Penguin Random House LLC.

The Cataloging-in-Publication Data is on file at the Library of Congress.

Vintage Classics Trade Paperback ISBN: 978-0-593-46756-5
eBook ISBN: 978-0-593-46757-2

vintagebooks.com

Printed in the United States of America
10 9 8 7 6 5 4 3 2 1

Contents

Introduction

Figlyarin, sitting at home, decided
That my black grandfather Gannibal
Was bought for a small jug of rum
And fell into some skipper's hands.

That skipper was the glorious skipper
By whom our country was set moving,
Who turned the rudder of our native ship
Forcefully onto its majestic course.
—Pushkin, from "My Genealogy," 1830[*]

Peter the Great (1672–1725), the last tsar and first emperor of Russia, was the "glorious skipper" who forcefully turned his country to the West, and in 1703, on a stretch of marshland facing the Gulf of Finland, began to build the city of St. Petersburg, giving Russia a major seaport open to Europe. "Finally Peter appeared . . . Russia entered Europe like a ship launched with the blow of an axe and the thunder of cannons." So Pushkin wrote in an unfinished essay entitled

---

[*] "Figlyarin," from the Russian word "figlyar" ("buffoon"), was Pushkin's play on the name of his enemy critic Faddei Bulgarin.

"On the Insignificance of Russian Literature" (1834). Pushkin was to play a similar role in that literature to the role Peter played in Russian history, and with as enduring an effect on its significance.

Throughout his work, Pushkin remained in complex relations with Peter: in his unfinished first novel, *The Moor of Peter the Great* (1828), portraying his black great-grandfather on his mother's side, Abram Petrovich Gannibal (1696–1781), the son of a Central African prince, who was captured by the Turks as a boy, sold into slavery, and then sent to Russia, where he was personally adopted by Peter (hence his patronym), and was eventually granted nobility and high military rank; in the narrative poem *Poltava* (1829), dealing with the decisive battle in which Peter's forces defeated the Swedish army and made Russia the leading nation of northern Europe; in his last long poem, *The Bronze Horseman* (1833), in which the mounted statue of Peter the Great on Senate Square in Petersburg comes ominously to life, at least in the deranged mind of the poem's hero, and goes galloping after him through the city.

Alexander Pushkin (1799–1837) was born a poet, but he became a master of prose and drama as well, and it was the body of his work as a whole that set Russian literature on its new course. In particular, he was intent on reforming Russian drama, a task he outlined in drafts of an introduction to his first play, *Boris Godunov*, and in an article "On National Drama," both written in 1829–1830 and both left unpublished. In the latter he raises the question directly:

Can our tragedy, formed on the example of Racinian tragedy, lose its aristocratic habits? How can it move from its measured, orderly, dignified, and polite dialogue to the crude frankness of popular passions, to the freedom of public-square opinions? How can it suddenly drop its obsequiousness, how can it do without the rules it is used to, without the forced accommodating of everything Russian to everything European; where, from whom can it learn an idiom comprehensible to the people? What are the passions of this people, what are the strings of its heart, where will it find resonance—in short, where are the spectators, where is the public?

Suggestions of an answer to these questions are given in the drafts for an introduction to *Boris Godunov*. The play was written in 1825, but not published until 1831, and not passed for performance by the theater censors until 1866, some thirty years after Pushkin's death. But he read the script to his friends, as he mentions in his notes, adding this enigmatic comment:

My tragedy is already known to almost all those whose opinion I value. From the number of my listeners there is one who was absent, the one to whom I owe the idea of my tragedy, whose genius inspired and sustained me, whose approval appeared to my imagination as the sweetest reward and was the only thing that diverted me in the midst of my solitary labor.

The absent one, left nameless here, is the poet, novelist, critic, and historian Nikolai Karamzin (1766–1826), whose twelve-volume *History of the Russian State*, elegantly written and rich in detail drawn from many years of research, was the first real account of Russia's complex past. Pushkin names him in the next part of the drafts:

> Studies of Shakespeare, Karamzin, and our old chronicles gave me the idea of clothing in dramatic forms one of the most dramatic epochs of recent history. Uninhibited by any other influence, I imitated Shakespeare in his free and broad portrayal of characters, in his loose and simple plot construction; I followed Karamzin in his lucid development of events; in the chronicles I tried to divine the way of thinking and the language of that time. Rich sources! Whether I made good use of them, I don't know—but in any case my labors were zealous and conscientious.

For Pushkin, the example of Shakespeare's theater, with its roots in the public square, not in courtly palaces, was essential to the reform of Russian drama, and in writing *Boris Godunov*, he acted on that belief. First of all, he replaced the French twelve-syllable alexandrine couplet, which had come to dominate Russian plays, with the iambic pentameter of English blank verse. But he went further than that, introducing vernacular prose in some scenes and playful rhyming in others, allowing for a great variety of voicing. He first referred to the play as a comedy, then came to call it a "romantic tragedy," but it more closely resembles Shakespeare's history plays in its composition and social inclusiveness. Even the comic passages are not there simply for entertainment; they also have their place in the historical drama. The drunken vagrant monks in the eighth scene, the foreign captains with their absurd accents in the sixteenth, the holy fool in the seventeenth—all cast their own light on the serious events of the play.[*] Then there are long monologues, brief scenes of pure action, candid personal exchanges, drama within drama—as in the superb thirteenth scene, the impostor's courtship of Marina Mnishek. The example of Shakespeare gave Pushkin an opening to this great variety.

The influence of the old chronicles is less obvious. Pushkin certainly studied them and drew details from them, but he did not imitate their language, as he seems to suggest. *Boris Godunov* is written in the natural living speech of his own time. He did, however, include a chronicler among his characters: the elderly monk Pimen of the fifth scene. Referring to him in a letter to the editor of *The Moscow Messenger* (1828), he wrote:

> The character of Pimen is not my invention. In him I have brought together the features that captivated me in our old chronicles: simpleheartedness, a touching meekness, something childish and at the same time wise, a zeal—one might say a pious zeal—for the God-given power of the tsars, a total absence of vanity, of partiality—all breathe in these precious memorials of times long past . . .

Pimen is a dramatic embodiment of the chroniclers. In his only scene, he sketches out the events of his final chronicle,

---

[*] The French captain Margeret was in fact a historical figure, as were the two characters named Pushkin.

which also happen to be the background of the play itself, and he converses with the young Grigory (Grishka) Otrepyev, who participated in the historical action and will become a major character in Pushkin's portrayal of it.

For the events of "one of the most dramatic epochs of recent history," his source, as he said, was Karamzin's *History of the Russian State*. Pushkin had met Nikolai Karamzin in 1816, while he was still studying at the imperial lycée in Tsarskoe Selo. At the time Karamzin had published only the first volume of his *History*, but by 1825, when Pushkin was writing *Boris Godunov*, eleven of the twelve volumes of the *History* had appeared. The events he chose to dramatize were drawn from the period known as the "Time of Troubles," which went from the death in 1598 of Fyodor I, the last tsar of the Rurik dynasty, to the accession in 1613 of Mikhail I, founder of the Romanov dynasty. During that fifteen-year interim, Russia had four tsars, two of whom were murdered and the last deposed; the first and longest-ruling was Boris Godunov himself.

Ivan the Terrible (he is referred to several times in the play as Ioann, and he and his grandfather, Ivan III, as "the two mighty Ioanns") inherited the title of Grand Prince of Moscow in 1533, at the age of three, and reigned as the first Tsar of All Russia from 1547 to 1584. At his death, his son Fyodor I (1557–1598) inherited the throne. Sometimes called Fyodor the Blessed, and referred to in Pushkin's play as "the angel-tsar," he was a pious and reclusive man who left most of the administrative duties to his brother-in-law, Boris Godunov. His marriage to Boris's sister Irina was childless, hence the "troubles" about the succession that followed his death. It is there that Pushkin begins his play.

The main trouble was that two years before the death of Ivan the Terrible, his fifth (some say seventh or even eighth) wife gave birth to a son, Dimitri, who was Fyodor's only brother. He was said to have died in childhood, but the question of his fate lingered on. It is raised in the opening scene, and his enigmatic absence/presence is the central question throughout the play. In the first version of the play, the closing line was the cry of the people: "Long live the tsar Dimitri Ivanovich!" The revised version, which we have followed, ends with a stage direction: "The people are silent." The change was made at the insistence of the emperor Nicholas I, for political reasons, but in fact it suits Pushkin's preference for ambiguity and unpredictability throughout the play. And the phrase itself soon became proverbial.

Pushkin did not continue his Shakespearean reform of Russian theater after *Boris Godunov*, though he originally had thoughts of writing two more plays dealing with the same historical period. His next major dramatic works, the four *Little Tragedies*, were written five years later and are very different both in style and conception. In 1825, however, he wrote the brief "Scene from *Faust*," first published in 1828 under the title "A New Scene Between Faust and Mephistopheles." Pushkin expressed great admiration for Goethe's *Faust*. In an unpublished note on Byron's tragedies, which he considered failed imitations of Goethe, he wrote: "*Faust* is the greatest creation of the poetic spirit; it serves as a representation of modern poetry, just as *The Iliad* serves as a monument of classical antiquity." But as the poet Gerard Manley Hopkins wrote to his friend the poet Robert Bridges in 1888: "The effect of studying masterpieces is to make me admire and do otherwise." So it was for Pushkin.

In "A Scene from *Faust*," there is none of Goethe's idealism. Faust declares to Mephistopheles that he is simply bored—and there is nothing metaphysical or romantic about his boredom. Mephistopheles, who is the main talker in the scene, latches on to that admission, since, as he confesses in the end, he is helpless on his own and depends on Faust to supply him with "little tasks." He is, in other words, a perfect embodiment of the banality of evil. Some readers have found the "Scene" the darkest, the most nihilistic of Pushkin's works, but that is to overlook the ambiguity of its tone, the comedy behind the darkness, and the artfulness of its rhyming iambic tetrameter.[*]

Boris Godunov and "A Scene from *Faust*" were the fruit of two years of "solitary labor" for Pushkin on his family estate of Mikhailovskoye, in the region of Pskov, close to the Estonian border. The solitude, however, was not of Pushkin's choosing. In fact, he was confined to the estate in 1824 on orders from the emperor Alexander I, because of his connection with certain political radicals of the time and his own satirical verses in support of them. But the confinement proved to be a productive period for Pushkin. Along with the plays, he collected and published his first book of short poems, finished his narrative poem *The Gypsies*, wrote two more narrative poems (*The Bridegroom* and *Count Nulin*), and worked on his novel in verse, *Evgeny Onegin*, completing the third chapter and adding three more.

Another benefit of his confinement was that it kept him from taking part in the Decembrist uprising in December

---

[*] In our translation, we have kept the meter but sacrificed the rhymes.

1825, following the sudden death of Alexander I, when some 3,000 rebellious troops refused to swear allegiance to Alexander's younger brother Nicholas. The uprising failed; five of the leaders were hanged, and many others were sent to hard labor in Siberia. Among them were a number of Pushkin's friends. When he was asked later by the emperor Nicholas I himself where he would have been on the day of the uprising, he replied candidly that he would have been on Senate Square with the rebels. Nicholas nevertheless released him from Mikhailovskoye, said that he could go wherever he liked and that he himself would be his censor. This imperial honor was not at all as flattering as Pushkin first took it to be. His real censor, as it turned out, was Count Alexander von Benckendorff, whom Nicholas had made the head of the newly organized Third Section, the secret police.

It was during another period of confinement that Pushkin wrote the *Little Tragedies*. This was in the autumn of 1830, when he was visiting his ancestral estate in the village of Boldino, in the Nizhny Novgorod region, some 385 miles east of Moscow. His father had made him a gift of the small estate in anticipation of his marriage to the young Natalya Goncharova, and in September he went to look it over. He meant to stay only a short time, but a cholera epidemic, which had been spreading from the east, struck the area during his visit, the roads were cordoned off, and he was quarantined on the estate for three months.

This period, known as the "Boldino Autumn," proved to be the most fruitful in his life. On December 9, 1830, soon after his return to Moscow, he wrote to his friend, the poet and critic Pyotr Alexandrovich Pletnev:

I'll tell you (in secret) that I wrote in Boldino as I haven't written for a long time. This is what I've brought back: the 2 *last* chapters of *Onegin*, the 8th and 9th, completely ready for print. A tale written in ottava rima (about 400 lines), which we'll bring out *Anonyme*. Several dramatic scenes, or little tragedies, namely: "The Miserly Knight," "Mozart and Salieri," "A Feast in a Time of Plague," and "Don Juan." On top of that I wrote some 30 short poems. Good? That's not all (a great secret).[*] I wrote 5 stories in prose, which make Baratynsky[†] hoot and holler—and which we'll also publish *Anonyme*.

Though the *Little Tragedies* are the contrary, artistically, of *Boris Godunov*, they continued Pushkin's exploration of dramatic forms outside the French neoclassical tradition. He had brought with him to Boldino a collection of contemporary works by English poets, including Barry Cornwall and John Wilson. Among the works of Cornwall, whose real name was Bryan Proctor (1787–1874), was a series of "Dramatic Scenes," published in 1817. The form itself interested Pushkin, though he did not borrow from Cornwall's scenes in writing his own. He did, however, borrow from *The City of the Plague*, a play by the Scottish poet and advocate John Wilson (1785–1854), first published in 1816, for the fourth of his little tragedies, *A Feast in a Time of Plague*. He took a single scene (act 1, scene 4) from Wilson's sprawling and wordy

---

[*] for you alone [Pushkin's note].

[†] Evgeny Baratynsky (1800–1844) was a poet in their circle. The stories were *The Tales of the Late Ivan Petrovich Belkin*, with Belkin presented as their author.

three-act drama and turned it into a twelve-page play—
a "little tragedy" indeed! Most of the dialogue in the *Feast*
is translated quite literally from Wilson's original, but the
two songs that are central to Pushkin's scene—Mary's lament
and Walsingham's hymn—are entirely his own.

The four *Little Tragedies* represent four different historical
periods and settings: *The Miserly Knight* is set in medieval
France, *Mozart and Salieri* in eighteenth-century Vienna,
The Stone Guest in seventeenth-century Madrid, and *A Feast
in a Time of Plague* in London during the Great Plague of
1665. For *The Miserly Knight*, Pushkin cites as a source
William Shenstone's tragicomedy *The Covetous Knight* (mis-
transcribing the poet's name as "Chenstone" and the title
as "The Cavetous Knight"). In fact, Shenstone, an English
poet and landscape gardener (1714–1763), wrote no such
play. It has been suggested that Pushkin used the "attribu-
tion" when he first published the play in 1836, in his maga-
zine *The Contemporary*, to forestall the notion that he might
be portraying his own strained relations with his father.
As for Mozart, the composer did have some complaints
about rivalry with his slightly older contemporary, Anto-
nio Salieri, when they were both working in Vienna, but
essentially they maintained a cool respect for each other. The
rumors on which *Mozart and Salieri* is based began to circulate only many years after Mozart's death. For the Don Juan
story, Pushkin had Molière's *Dom Juan ou le festin de pierre*
(1665) and Mozart's *Don Giovanni* (1787) as predecessors.
He seems not to have known the first Don Juan drama, *The
Trickster of Seville and the Stone Guest*, by Tirso de Molina
(1579–1648).

What matters, however, is not the sources but the way

Pushkin used them. He "parodied literature with the voice of life," as Andrei Sinyavsky puts it in his *Strolls with Pushkin*.[*] The phrase goes to the essence of the *Little Tragedies*. The first three might be taken as morality plays on the cardinal sins of greed, envy, and lust. But the closer we look, the more complicated the morality becomes, the more profound the human complexity of the characters, for all the brevity of their moments onstage. The sudden ending of *The Miserly Knight* does not round off the story of the baron's son; in *Mozart and Salieri*, the curtain falls on Salieri's unanswered question, essentially about himself; the abrupt resolution of *The Stone Guest* leaves Doña Anna abandoned; and Walsingham, who defiantly sings in praise of the Plague, remains "sunk in deep thought" at the end. The conflicts are not resolved; they are suspended. The effect is to make us go back and search for what we might have missed. And that search reveals more and more of the inner life of the characters implicit in the brief "dramatic scenes."

The Water Nymph (*Rusalka* in Russian), written in 1832, was Pushkin's last play, and here, too, the action is abruptly broken off. It seems he simply never finished it, but as John Bayley notes in his commentary, "In a sense it is a highly Pushkinian ending, to leave the rest to our imagination."[†] Water nymphs were well known in European folklore. They generally had a rather playful and seductive nature, but on the banks of the Dnieper they acquired a darker character. Pushkin also gives his heroine a personal and very real human

[*] Translated by Catharine Theimer Nepomnyashchy and Slava I. Yastremski (New York: Columbia University Press, 2017), 63.
[†] John Bayley, *Pushkin: A Comparative Commentary* (New York: Cambridge University Press, 1971), 234.

drama in her relations with her father and the prince that goes well beyond folklore. Her wish for vengeance does not come merely from a nymph's innate wickedness.

We meet this combination of folktale or parable and underlying human drama again in the last work included here: the narrative/drama *Angelo*, written in 1833, drawn from Shakespeare's *Measure for Measure*, one of his late "problem plays." Here Pushkin goes back to Shakespeare in a more literal sense than when he began; in fact, it seems he had been toying with translating Shakespeare's play before he turned to the hybrid form he settled on, and most of the dramatic sections of *Angelo* are taken directly from *Measure for Measure*. But as with his earlier borrowings, Pushkin has radically condensed the original from a full five acts to 535 lines, eliminating the many secondary characters and all of the low comic business. He also shifts the setting from Shakespeare's Vienna to "happy Italy." At the same time, he reinstates the formal rhymed alexandrines that he initially rejected for blank verse (and which we have not attempted to keep in our translation).

"Pushkin thought mainly in fragments," Sinyavsky wrote.* "That was his style." So we have "A Scene from *Faust*," the *Little Tragedies*, the sudden ending of *The Water Nymph* just as the prince literally faces the consequences of his actions, the swift and merciful resolution of *Angelo*. In a sense even *Boris Godunov* is a fragment: "The people are silent." But the silence resonates.

—Richard Pevear

---

* *Strolls with Pushkin*, 69.

Boris Godunov

(1824–1825)

To the memory, precious for the Russian people, of
NIKOLAI MIKHAILOVICH KARAMZIN
Alexander Pushkin dedicates this work, inspired by his genius,
with reverence and gratitude

KREMLIN PALACE

February 20, 1598

Princes Shuisky and Vorotynsky

VOROTYNSKY

We were dispatched to keep watch on the city,
But it looks like there is no one to be seen;
Moscow is empty; the people have all left,
Following the patriarch* to the monastery.
How do you think this turbulence will end?

SHUISKY

How will it end? That isn't hard to guess:
The people will go on with their tears and howls,
Boris will go on wincing for a while,
As drunkards do over a glass of vodka,
And finally, out of kindness,
He will humbly agree to take the crown;
And then—and then he will rule over us
As before.

---

* There is a glossary of Russian titles and terms at the end of the play.

VOROTYNSKY

But a month has already gone by
Since he withdrew into his sister's convent,
As if to abandon all that's worldly.
Neither the patriarch nor the assembled boyars
Have managed to persuade him otherwise;
He doesn't heed their tearful admonitions,
Nor their pleas, nor the weeping of all Moscow,
Nor the voice of the Great Council. In vain
They've pleaded with his sister to bless Boris
As their ruler; the mournful nun-tsaritsa
Is as firm as he, and as implacable.
Boris must have instilled this spirit in her;
What if the regent himself indeed
Is weary of the cares of ruling and refuses
To mount the empty throne? What would you say?

SHUISKY

I would say the blood of the young tsarevich
Has been spilled to no purpose; that in that case
Dimitri could still be alive.

VOROTYNSKY

Terrible villainy!
Did Boris really kill the tsarevich?

SHUISKY

Who else?
Who made vain attempts to bribe Chepchugov?
Who sent the two Bityagovskys and Kachalov
To Uglich? I was sent there myself
To investigate the matter in place: I found

Fresh tracks; the whole town witnessed the villainy;
The citizens all gave the same testimony;
And on my return I could well have exposed
The underhanded villain with a single word.

VOROTYNSKY
Then why didn't you destroy him on the spot?

SHUISKY
I must confess, he confused me at the time
By his calm, by his unexpected shamelessness.
He looked me in the eye like an honest man,
Asked questions, went into small details—
And before him I repeated the absurdity
That he himself insinuated.

VOROTYNSKY
                    Not good, Prince.

SHUISKY
What was I to do? Announce it all
To Fyodor? But the tsar looked at everything
With Godunov's eyes, heard everything with Godunov's ears:
If I persuaded him of it all, Boris
Would instantly unpersuade him, and then
They would send me packing off to prison,
And with God's help would quietly strangle me
In a remote cell, as they did my uncle.
I'm not boasting, and if it so happens,
I have no fear of any punishment,
I'm not a coward, but I'm also not so stupid
As to put my neck in a noose for no good reason.

VOROTYNSKY

Terrible villainy! But listen: surely
The murderer is troubled by remorse:
Of course, the blood of the innocent child prevents him
From taking the throne.

SHUISKY

He will get over it;
Boris isn't timid! What an honor
For us, for all of Russia! Yesterday's slave,
A Tartar, Malyuta's son-in-law, the son-in-law
Of an executioner, and he, too, in his soul,
An executioner, will take upon himself
The crown and the mantle of Monomakh . . .

VOROTYNSKY

Yes, he's not of noble birth; we are more noble.

SHUISKY

So it seems.

VOROTYNSKY

Why, Shuisky, Vorotynsky . . .
To say the least, we are of princely birth.

SHUISKY

Of princely birth, and of the blood of Rurik.

VOROTYNSKY

And listen, Prince, we could well have the right
To inherit from Fyodor.

SHUISKY

Yes, far more right

Than Godunov.

VOROTYNSKY

Indeed we do!

SHUISKY

What then?

If Boris doesn't stop his trickery,
We can cleverly stir the people up
And get them to abandon Godunov.
They have enough of their own princes, let them
Elect any one of them to be their tsar.

VOROTYNSKY

We're not few, the Varangians' descendants,
But it's hard for us to vie with Godunov:
The people aren't used to seeing us as heirs
Of their ancient warlords. We lost our domains
Long ago, we have long served the tsars
As retinue, while he knew how
To beguile the people with fear and love and glory.

SHUISKY

(looking out the window)

He's bold, that's all—while we . . . but enough. Look,
The people are coming back in scattered groups.
Let's go quickly and find out what's decided.

RED SQUARE
The People

ONE

He is implacable! He drove away
The bishops, the boyars, and the patriarch.
In vain did they prostrate themselves before him;
He cannot bear the glory of the throne.

ANOTHER

Oh, Lord God, who will rule over us?
Oh, woe to us!

A THIRD

Here is the chief clerk
Come to tell us the decision of the Duma.

PEOPLE

Quiet! Quiet! The Duma clerk will speak;
Shh—listen!

SHCHELKALOV

(from the Red Porch)

Together we have decided
To try for a last time the power of a plea
Over the grief-stricken soul of our ruler.
Tomorrow morning the most holy patriarch,
After a solemn prayer service in the Kremlin,
Will set out with holy banners and with icons
Of Our Lady of Vladimir and of the Don,
And with him the council, the boyars, the host
Of nobles, the elected townsmen, and all
The Orthodox people of Moscow—we will all go
And plead again with the tsaritsa
To have pity on orphaned Moscow and to bless
Boris with the crown. Now go with God
Back to your homes, and pray that the zealous
Orthodox prayer will rise up to heaven.

The people disperse.

MAIDEN FIELD
The New Maiden Convent
The People

ONE

Now they've gone to the tsaritsa's cell.
Boris and the patriarch went inside
With a throng of boyars.

ANOTHER

Any word?

A THIRD

                       He still
Resists; but there's some hope.

WOMAN

(with a baby)

                    Goo, goo! Don't cry,
Here comes the bogeyman, the bogeyman will snatch you!
Goo, goo! . . . don't cry!

ONE

Can't we get past the fence?

ANOTHER

We can't. No way! And even the field is packed,
Not only there. Look! The whole of Moscow
Is crammed in here; see: the fence, the roofs,
All the tiers of the cathedral belfry,
The church domes and the very crosses
Are studded with people.

FIRST

A pretty sight!

ONE

What's that noise there?

ANOTHER

Listen! What's that noise?
The people are wailing, they're falling down like waves,
Row after row . . . more . . . more . . . Well, brother,
It's our turn; quick now! get on your knees!

THE PEOPLE
(on their knees, weeping and wailing)
Ah, have mercy, father! rule over us!
Be our father, our tsar!

ONE
(in a low voice)
Why are they weeping?

ANOTHER

How should we know? That's the boyars' business,
Not for our kind.

WOMAN
(with baby)
So when you ought to cry,
You're quiet! I'll show you! Here's the bogeyman!
Cry, you spoiled brat!
(She throws him on the ground. The baby squeals.)
So there.

ONE
They're all crying,
Let us cry, too, brother.

ANOTHER
I'm trying, brother,
But I can't.

THE FIRST
Neither can I. Do you have an onion?
We could rub our eyes.

THE SECOND
No, I'll smear them with spit.
What else is happening?

FIRST
Who can tell with them?

THE PEOPLE

The crown is his! He's the tsar! He has agreed!
Boris is our tsar! Long live Boris!

KREMLIN PALACE

Boris, the Patriarch, Boyars

BORIS

You, Father Patriarch, and all of you boyars,
My soul is laid bare before you: you have seen
With what awe and humility I accept
This great power. How heavy is my duty!
The heir of the two mighty Ioanns—
The heir, too, of the angel-tsar! . . .
O righteous man! O my sovereign father!
Look down from heaven on the tears of your faithful
    servants
And send your holy blessing upon the one you loved,
Whom you have so wondrously elevated here:
That I may rule my people in glory, that I
May be as good and righteous as you were.
From you I expect assistance, my boyars,
Serve me as you formerly served him,
When I, too, had a share in your same labors,
Before I was chosen by the people's will.

BOYARS

We won't betray the oath we've given you.

BORIS

Let us go now, bow down before the graves
Of the late rulers of Russia, and then summon
All our people to the banquet, all
From the highest lords to the last blind beggar;
Let all enter freely, all are our dear guests.

He exits, followed by the boyars.

PRINCE VOROTYNSKY
(holding Shuisky back)

You guessed right.

SHUISKY

What?

VOROTYNSKY

Here, today,
Don't you remember?

SHUISKY

No, I remember nothing.

VOROTYNSKY

When the people went out to the Maiden Field,
You said . . .

SHUISKY

Now is no time for remembering,
And I advise you to forget sometimes.
In fact I merely wished to test you then

With feigned slander, so as to learn for certain
Your secret thoughts; but look now—the people
Are greeting the tsar—my absence may be noticed—
I will follow him.

VOROTYNSKY
Crafty courtier!

NIGHT.
A CELL IN THE CHUDOV MONASTERY.

1603

Father Pimen, Grigory (asleep)

PIMEN

(writing in front of a lamp)

One more, one last story, and my chronicle
Is finished, the duty God imposed on me, a sinner,
Is fulfilled. Not for nothing did the Lord
Make me a witness of so many years
And instill in me the art of writing;
Someday an assiduous monk will find
My diligent nameless work, will light his lamp
As I do now, and shaking the dust of time
From these pages, copy out my truthful stories,
So that the descendants of the Orthodox
May know the past life of their native land,
Remember the great tsars, their works, their glory,
Their goodness—and humbly pray the Savior
To forgive them for their sins and their dark deeds.
In my old age I live again, the past

Emerges before me—was it long ago
That it raced by, filled with events, surging
Like the ocean? Now it is still and calm,
Few are the faces my memory has kept,
Few are the words that reach me now, the rest
Is gone forever . . . But dawn is near, the lamp
Is dying down—just one more, one last story.

He writes.

GRIGORY
(*waking up*)

That same dream—can it be?—for the third time!
A cursed dream! . . . And the old man still sits
By the lamp and writes—and nods his head,
Which means he hasn't shut his eyes all night.
How I love his peaceful look as he goes on
With his chronicles, his soul immersed in the past,
And I have often tried to guess
What he was writing about: the dark rule
Of the Tartars? The atrocious executions of Ioann?
The stormy assemblies of Novgorod?
The glory of the fatherland? In vain.
It was impossible to read his hidden thoughts
Either in his high brow or in his gaze;
It was ever the same humble, dignified look.
Just so a clerk grown white-haired in the court
Looks calmly at the innocent and the guilty,
Hearing impassively both good and evil,
Knowing neither pity nor wrath.

PIMEN

You're awake, brother.

GRIGORY

Bless me, righteous Father.

PIMEN

May the blessing of the Lord be upon you
Now and ever and unto ages of ages.

GRIGORY

You went on writing and didn't fall asleep,
While a demonic reverie disturbed my peace,
And the fiend confused me. In my dream
A steep stairway led me up a tower.
From its height I saw Moscow like an anthill.
The square down below teemed with people,
And they pointed at me and laughed,
And I was ashamed and became all frightened,
And falling down headlong, I awoke . . .
The same dream repeated itself three times.
Isn't that strange?

PIMEN

Your young blood is stirring.
Calm yourself with prayer and with fasting,
And light visions will fill your dreams. Even now,
If I'm overcome by involuntary slumber
And do not say a long evening prayer,
My old man's sleep is not quiet and not sinless,
I imagine noisy banquets, war camps, battles,
And all the wild dreams of those young years!

GRIGORY

Ah, how happily you spent your youth!
You fought beneath the battlements of Kazan,
You beat back the Lithuanians under Shuisky,
You saw the court and splendor of Ioann!
What luck! While I, ever since my boyhood years,
Have wandered from cell to cell as a poor monk!
Why couldn't I, too, taste the joys of battle,
Or feast at the banquets of the tsar?
I'd have had time, like you, in my old age,
To lay aside vanity and worldliness,
Take monastic vows,
And shut myself up in a quiet hermitage.

PIMEN

Don't complain, brother, that early on
You left the sinful world, that the Almighty
Sent you so few temptations. Believe you me:
It's from afar that we're seduced by fame,
And luxury, and women's deceitful love.
I have lived long and known many delights,
But I have known bliss only since the time
The Lord brought me to the monastery.
Think, my son, think about great tsars.
Who is higher? Only God. Who dares
To oppose them? No one. What then? Often
The golden crown weighed heavy on their heads;
They exchanged it for a monk's hood. Tsar Ioann
Sought peace in a semblance of monastic tasks.
His palace, filled with his proud favorites,
Acquired the new look of a monastery:

His guardsmen, wearing skullcaps and hair shirts,
Turned into obedient monks, and the terrible
Tsar himself became a humble abbot.
I saw here, in this very cell
(The much-suffering Kirill lived in it then,
A righteous man. By then God had allowed me
To perceive the worthlessness of worldly vanity),
Here I saw the tsar
Weary of wrathful thoughts and executions.
Pensive, quiet, the Terrible sat with us,
We stood motionless before him, and he
Spoke softly with us. He said to the abbot and brothers:
"My Fathers, the longed-for day will come
When I stand here thirsting for salvation.
You, Nikodim, you, Sergei, you, Kirill,
You all—receive my spiritual vow:
I, a cursed criminal, will come to you
And will be honorably tonsured here,
Falling down, holy Father, at your feet."
So spoke the all-powerful sovereign,
And the speech flowed sweetly from his lips.
And he wept. And we, in tears, prayed
That the Lord God would send down love and peace
Upon his suffering and stormy soul.
And his son Fyodor? On his throne he pined
For the peaceful, silent life of a recluse.
He transformed the palace into a prayerful cell;
There the weighty cares of sovereignty
Did not disturb his saintly soul. God loved
The tsar's humility, and in his time
Russia enjoyed its glory undisturbed—

And an unheard-of miracle took place
At the hour of his death:
A man of astonishingly bright appearance
Came to the tsar's bed, seen by him alone,
And Fyodor began to talk with him and called him
Great patriarch. And everyone around
Was seized with fear, realizing that it was
A heavenly vision, since the holy patriarch
Was not there in the house before the tsar.
And when he passed away, the rooms were filled
With holy fragrance, his face shone like the sun—
We will not see a tsar like him again.
O terrible, unprecedented grief!
We've angered God, we've sinned, we have appointed
A regicide as our ruler.

GRIGORY
I've long meant
To ask you, venerable Father, about the death
Of the tsarevich Dimitri; at that time
They say you were in Uglich.

PIMEN
Ah, I remember it!
God granted me to see that evil deed,
That bloody sin. I was sent to far-off Uglich
As an obedience; I arrived at night.
In the morning, at the hour of the liturgy,
I suddenly hear ringing, the sound of an alarm,
Shouting, noise. Everybody runs
To the tsaritsa's quarters. I rush there, too—
The whole town is already there. I look.

The murdered tsarevich is lying on the ground,
The mother tsaritsa, beside herself, bends over him,
The wet nurse is wailing in despair.
Then frenzied people come, dragging with them
The godless, treacherous nanny . . .
Suddenly among them, fierce, pale with wrath,
Appears the Judas, Bityagovsky. "He,
He is the villain!"—comes the general cry,
And in an instant he's no more. Then the people
Rushed after the three fleeing murderers;
The villains were taken in their hiding place
And brought before the child's still-warm body,
And—O wonder!—suddenly the dead boy trembled.
"Confess!" the people shouted at them:
And in terror of the axe, the villains
Confessed—and named Boris.

GRIGORY

How old was the murdered tsarevich?

PIMEN

                       About seven;
He would now be (it happened ten . . . no, more:
Twelve years ago)—he would be your age
And on the throne; but God chose otherwise.
With this sorrowful account I will conclude
My chronicle; since then I have entered little
Into worldly affairs. Brother Grigory,
You have enlightened your mind with literacy,
I hand my work over to you. In the hours
Free of spiritual endeavors, describe quite simply
Everything you witness in your life:

War and peace, the rule of the sovereigns,
The holy miracles of saintly men,
The prophecies and signs from heaven—
For me it's time, it's long since time to rest
And put out my lamp . . . The bell rings for the liturgy . . .
Bless, Lord, Thy servants! . . . Hand me my crutch, Grigory.

He exits.

GRIGORY

Boris, Boris! everything trembles before you,
No one dares remind you of the poor child's fate—
And meanwhile the recluse here in his dark cell
Is writing a terrible denunciation of you:
And you will not escape the world's judgment
Any more than you will escape the judgment of God.

THE PATRIARCH'S PALACE

The Patriarch and the Superior of the Chudov Monastery

PATRIARCH

So he fled, Father Superior?

SUPERIOR

He did, Your Holiness. Three days ago.

PATRIARCH

The damned rogue! What is his ancestry?

SUPERIOR

He's from the Otrepyevs, offspring of Galician boyars.
He was tonsured at an early age, no one knows where,
lived in Suzdal, in the St. Euphemius Monastery, left it,
hung around in several other monasteries, finally came to
my Chudov brethren, and seeing he was still young and
unformed, I placed him under the guidance of Father Pimen,
a meek and humble elder; and he became quite literate:
he read our chronicles, composed canons for the saints;
but evidently his literacy did not come to him from God . . .

PATRIARCH

These literate ones! What nonsense it all is! *I will rule in Moscow!* Ah, a diabolic vessel! No need to report it to the tsar, however; why trouble our sovereign father? It would be enough to report the fugitive to the clerk Smirnov or the clerk Efimyev. What a heresy! *I will rule in Moscow! . . .* Catch him, catch the fiend-pleaser, and send him off to the Solovetsky Monastery for eternal penance. This is a heresy, Father Superior.

SUPERIOR

A heresy, Holy Master, a downright heresy.

THE TSAR'S PALACE
Two Courtiers

FIRST
Where is the sovereign?

SECOND
            In his bedchamber.
He's locked himself up with some sorcerer or other.

FIRST
Yes, that's become his favorite conversation:
Wizards, diviners, sorcerers—
He keeps at the fortune-telling like a young bride.
I wish I knew what he wants to divine.

SECOND
Here he comes. Would you like to ask him?

FIRST
How grim he looks!

They exit.

TSAR

(enters)

I have reached the highest power;
For six years now I have reigned peacefully.
But there's no happiness in my soul. Is it not
The same for me as for some amorous youth
Who desires the joys of love, but the heart's hunger
Is no sooner sated with momentary possession
Than he turns cold, is bored and languishes? . . .
In vain do the wizards promise me long days,
Days of untroubled rule—neither power nor life
Bring me any joy; I can sense the coming
Of thunder from heaven and woe.
For me there is no happiness. I thought
To placate my people with rewards, with honor,
To win their love with generosity—
But I gave up that meaningless endeavor:
Living power is hateful to the mob,
They know only how to love the dead.
We are mad to let our hearts be troubled
By the people's praise or by their cries of fury!
God sent famine upon our land,
The people wailed and died in agony;
I opened granaries for them, I poured out
Gold before them, and I found them work—
Yet they cursed me in their rage! Fires
Destroyed their homes, I built new lodgings for them.
Yet they blamed me for the fires! That
Is how the mob judges: go seek their love.
I hoped to find comfort in my family,
I hoped to see my daughter happily married—

Like a storm, death carried off her bridegroom . . .
And then rumor deviously calls
Me, me, the wretched father,
The cause of my own daughter's widowhood! . . .
Whoever dies, it is I who secretly killed them:
I hastened the demise of Fyodor, poisoned my sister,
The tsaritsa, a humble nun . . . I did it all!
Ah, I feel nothing can bring us peace
Amid these worldly sorrows; nothing, nothing . . .
Maybe only conscience. If it is sound,
It will triumph over malice and dark slander—
But if a single stain, a single one,
Happens to be found on it—disaster!
Like a pestilence, it burns your soul,
It fills your heart with poison, its reproach
Hammers in your ears, and you are nauseous,
And your head spins, and there are bloodied boys
Before your eyes . . . You would be glad to flee,
But there is nowhere . . . Ah, how terrible!
Woe to the man whose conscience is not clean.

A TAVERN ON THE LITHUANIAN BORDER

Misail and Varlaam, vagrant monks;
Grigory Otrepyev, in civilian dress; the hostess

HOSTESS

What can I offer you, honorable elders?

VARLAAM

Whatever God sends, dear hostess. Might there be some drink?

HOSTESS

How could there not be, my Fathers! I'll bring it at once.

She exits.

MISAIL

Why so woebegone, my friend? We're at the Lithuanian border, which you were so anxious to reach.

GRIGORY

I won't be at peace till I'm in Lithuania.

VARLAAM

Wherefore such love for Lithuania? Look at us,
Father Misail and me, a sinner: once we fled from the
monastery, we didn't give a thought to anything. Litva,
Rus, a gander, a goose: it's all the same to us, provided
there's drink . . . and it's here in a wink! . . .

MISAIL

Nicely rhymed, Father Varlaam.

HOSTESS
(enters)
Here you are, my Fathers. Good health to you.

MISAIL

Thank you, dear, God bless you.

*The monks drink; Varlaam strikes up a song: "In the city of
Kazan . . ."*

VARLAAM
(to Grigory)
Why don't you cheer up or drink up?

GRIGORY

I don't want to.

MISAIL

A free man's as free . . .

VARLAAM

As a drunkard on a spree, Father Misail! Let's drink a little
glass to the bartender lass . . . However, Father Misail,
when I drink, I think the sober stink; it's one thing to be
a sot and another to be a snot; if you want to live like us,

you're welcome—if not, clear out, get lost: a clown's no
friend to a priest.

GRIGORY

Drink, but also think, Father Varlaam! You see, I, too, can
rhyme nicely.

VARLAAM

And what am I to think about?

MISAIL

Let him be, Father Varlaam.

VARLAAM

Just look at his lenten mug! He foisted himself on our
company, but who is he, where is he from—and he's
arrogant at that: maybe he's had a taste of the rack . . .

He drinks and sings: "A young fellow got himself tonsured . . ."

GRIGORY
(to the hostess)
Where does this road lead?

HOSTESS

To Lithuania, my provider, to the Luevy Hills.

GRIGORY

Is it far to these Luevy Hills?

HOSTESS

Not far, you could make it by nightfall, if it weren't for the
tsar's barriers and sentry patrols.

GRIGORY

Barriers! What's that about?

HOSTESS

Someone has fled from Moscow, and there's an order to
detain and examine everybody.

GRIGORY

(to himself)

Well, here we go!

VARLAAM

Eh, friend! You've already sidled up to the hostess.
Meaning drink's not what you need, but a girl of good
breed. Really, brother, really! Each of us has his own way;
me and Father Misail have one little task: to finish the flask;
we drink, turn it over, and ask for another.

MISAIL

Nicely rhymed, Father Varlaam.

GRIGORY

Who is it they're after? Who fled from Moscow?

HOSTESS

God alone knows, maybe a thief, a robber—only nowadays
even good people don't have free passage. And what will
it come to? Nothing. The devil they'll catch anybody; as if
there's no other way to Lithuania than the highway! Just
turn left from here, go down the path through the forest to
the chapel on the Chekan brook, then straight across the
swamp to Khlopino, from there to Zakharyevo, and there
any little boy will take you to the Luevy Hills. All these
sentries do is harass passersby and fleece poor folk.

Noise is heard.

HOSTESS

What's that now? Ah, here they come, the fiends! Making
their rounds.

GRIGORY

Hostess! Is there some dark corner in the cottage?

HOSTESS

No, there isn't, my dear. I'd be glad to hide myself.
They say they're just making their rounds, but I have
to give them drink and bread and God knows what—
may they all drop dead, damn them! May they . . .

The patrol enters.

PATROLMAN

Greetings, hostess!

HOSTESS

Welcome, dear guests, please come in . . .

PATROLMAN
(to another patrolman)

Hah! they're having a spree: we can cash in on it. *(to the
monks)* Who are you people?

VARLAAM

We're God's elders, humble monks. We go around the
villages collecting alms from Christians for our monastery.

PATROLMAN
(to Grigory)

And you?

MISAIL

He's our companion . . .

GRIGORY

I'm a layman from the outskirts; I brought the elders to the border, and I'll be going back to my place now.

MISAIL

So you've changed your . . .

GRIGORY
(aside)

Quiet.

PATROLMAN

Hostess, bring us more drink—we'll have a sip with the elders here and talk with them.

ANOTHER PATROLMAN
(aside)

The lad seems to be a pauper—we won't make anything from him—but the elders . . .

FIRST

Quiet, we'll get at them now. —Well, Fathers, how's it going?

VARLAAM

Poorly, my son, poorly! Christian folk are stingy these days; they love money, they hide money. They give little to God. A great sinfulness has come upon the peoples of the earth. They've all turned mercenary, money-grubbing; they think about worldly riches and not about saving their souls. We go around, go around; beg, beg; sometimes we don't get three pennies in three days. Such sinfulness! A week goes by, another, you peek into your purse—there's so little in it that it's shameful to show your face in the monastery. What can you do? In your grief you go and drink away what's left; it's

just terrible. —Ah, it's so bad, it must be our last days have
come . . .

HOSTESS

(weeps)

Lord, have mercy and save us!

During Varlaam's speech, the first patrolman peers intently at
Misail.

FIRST PATROLMAN

Alyokha! Have you got the tsar's order with you?

SECOND

Yes.

FIRST

Give it to me.

MISAIL

Why are you staring at me like that?

FIRST PATROLMAN

Here's why: a certain wicked heretic has fled from Moscow—
Grishka Otrepyev—have you heard about it?

MISAIL

No, I haven't.

PATROLMAN

You haven't? Very well. And the tsar has ordered that this
fled heretic be caught and hung. Do you know that?

MISAIL

No, I don't.

PATROLMAN
(to Varlaam)

Do you know how to read?

VARLAAM

I did when I was young, but now I've forgotten.

PATROLMAN
(to Misail)

And you?

MISAIL

The Lord didn't teach me.

PATROLMAN

So here is the tsar's order for you.

MISAIL

Why for me?

PATROLMAN

It seems to me that this fled heretic, thief, swindler—
is you.

MISAIL

Me?! Good lord, what are you saying?

PATROLMAN

Wait! Block the door! Now we'll deal with him.

HOSTESS

Ah, the cursed tormentors! They won't leave an old man in
peace!

PATROLMAN

Who here can read?

GRIGORY
(*stepping forward*)

I can.

PATROLMAN

Well, now! And who did you learn from?

GRIGORY

Our sexton.

PATROLMAN
(*hands him the order*)

Read it aloud.

GRIGORY
(*reads*)

"The unworthy monk of the Chudov Monastery, Grigory, of
the Otrepyev family, fell into heresy and, instructed by the
devil, made so bold as to stir up the holy brotherhood by
all sorts of temptations and lawlessness. Our investigation
shows that this fiend, Grishka, fled toward the Lithuanian
border . . ."

PATROLMAN
(*to Misail*)

Who else if not you?

GRIGORY

"And the tsar ordered him caught . . ."

PATROLMAN

And hung.

GRIGORY

Here it doesn't say "hung."

PATROLMAN

Nonsense: you don't have to write out every word.
Read: "caught and hung."

GRIGORY

"And hung. This thief Grishka is . . ." (*looks at Varlaam*)
"over fifty. Of medium height, bald brow, gray beard, fat
belly . . ."

They all look at Varlaam.

FIRST PATROLMAN

Boys, this is Grishka! Hold him, bind him! Who would
have thought it?!

VARLAAM
(*snatches the order*)

Back off, you sons of bitches! What kind of Grishka am
I? So! Over fifty, gray beard, fat belly! No, brother, you're
too young to make fun of me! It's been a while since I read
anything, but if it's a matter of the noose, I'll figure it out.
(*Reads slowly*) "He is . . . twenty years old." So, brothers,
where's this fifty? See, it says "twenty."

SECOND PATROLMAN

Yes, I remember, twenty. That's what they told us.

FIRST PATROLMAN
(*to Grigory*)

So, brother, it seems you're a joker.

*During the reading Grigory stands with his head lowered, his
hand in his bosom.*

VARLAAM

(continues)

"Of small stature, broad-chested, one arm shorter than the other, blue eyes, red hair, a wart on his cheek, another on his forehead." But isn't that you, friend?

Grigory suddenly pulls out a dagger; everyone steps back; he throws himself out the window.

PATROLMEN

Seize him! Seize him!

They all rush about in disorder.

MOSCOW. SHUISKY'S HOUSE.
Shuisky, many guests. Supper.

SHUISKY

More wine.

He stands up; they all do the same.

           Well, my dear guests,
This is the last cup. Read the prayer, boy.

BOY

King of Heaven, who art ever and everywhere,
Heed the humble prayer of thy servants:
We pray for our sovereign, thy chosen one,
The pious, autocratic ruler of all Christians.
Safeguard him in his palace, on the road,
On the battlefield, and in the bed of sleep.
Grant him victory over his enemies,
And let him be glorified from sea to sea.
May his family flourish in good health,
And may its precious branches spread

The whole world over—and to us, his servants,
May he be always benevolent, and merciful,
And long-suffering, and may the sources
Of his boundless wisdom pour down on us.
To this we raise our cup, and for our king
We pray to thee who art the King of Heaven.

SHUISKY
(drinks)

Long live our great sovereign!
And to you, dear guests, I say goodbye;
I thank you that you've chosen not to scorn
My hospitality. Goodbye and sleep well.

The guests leave. He accompanies them to the door.

PUSHKIN

They're gone at last. Well, Prince Vassily Ivanovich, I
thought we wouldn't have a chance to talk.

SHUISKY
(to the servants)

What are you gaping at? All you want to do is eavesdrop.
Clear the table and get out. What is it, Afanasy
Mikhailovich?

PUSHKIN

Wonders never cease.
Today my nephew, Gavrila Pushkin,
Sent me a messenger from Kraków.

SHUISKY
Well?

PUSHKIN

It is strange news my nephew writes to me.
The Terrible's son . . . Wait.

He goes to the door and looks around.

The sovereign youth
Was murdered on Boris's orders . . .

SHUISKY

That is no news.

PUSHKIN

But wait a moment: Dimitri is alive.

SHUISKY

Well, now! That is news! The tsarevich is alive!
That is truly a wonder. And is that all?

PUSHKIN

Listen to the end. Whoever he may be,
The saved tsarevich, or some spirit in his image,
Or a bold trickster, a shameful impostor—
In any case Dimitri appeared there.

SHUISKY

It can't be.

PUSHKIN

Pushkin himself saw him,
Coming to the palace for the first time,
And walking through ranks of Lithuanian lords
Straight to the private chambers of the king.

SHUISKY

But who is he? Where from?

PUSHKIN

                    Nobody knows.
What is known is that he had been a servant
To Vishnevetsky, that on his sickbed
He revealed himself to a confessor,
That the proud lord, having learned the secret,
Looked after him, brought him back to health,
And then went with him to King Sigismund.

SHUISKY

What do they say about this clever fellow?

PUSHKIN

One hears he's smart, amiable, adroit,
Liked by everybody. He has charmed
The Moscow refugees. Latin priests support him.
The king showers him with favors and, they say,
Has promised to help him.

SHUISKY

                    That's all such mayhem, brother,
That one's head starts to spin despite itself.
There is no doubt that he is an impostor,
But, I admit, the danger's not a small one.
The news is important! And if it should reach
The people, there will be a great upheaval.

PUSHKIN

Such an upheaval, it's unlikely Tsar Boris
Will keep the crown upon his clever head.
And he has it coming! He rules over us

Like the tsar Ivan (a name that gives us nightmares).
True, there are no outright executions;
True, we don't sing hymns to the Lord Jesus
On a bloody stake, in front of all the people;
True, we are not burnt alive on the square,
While the tsar stirs the hot coals with his staff.
But are we so certain of our own poor lives?
We can expect disgrace at any moment.
Prison, Siberia, a monk's hood, or chains,
And there, in the wilds, a hungry death or a noose.
Where are the noblest families among us?
Where are the Sitsky princes, the Shestunovs,
The Romanovs, the hope of the fatherland?
They are in prison, they are rotting in exile.
Just you wait: your lot will be the same.
Think a minute! In our homes we're besieged
By faithless knaves, as if by Lithuanians,
All of them spies, ready to sell us out,
Thieves bought and paid for by the government.
We're dependent on the first flunky
That we're intent on punishing. Just look—
He decided to abolish St. George's Day.
We have no power on our own estates.
We don't dare to drive out a lazy oaf.
Like it or not, feed him; do not dare
To lure away other workers! —Or it's the law.
Were such evils heard of even under Tsar Ivan?
And is it easier for the people? Ask them.
The impostor need only promise to restore
The old St. George's Day. Then the fun will start.

SHUISKY

You're right, Pushkin. But do you know what?
Let's be quiet about it for now.

PUSHKIN

Of course,
We'll keep it to ourselves. You're a smart man;
I'm always glad to talk things over with you,
And if occasionally something troubles me,
I cannot help confiding it to you.
Besides, today your mead and mellow beer
Really loosened my tongue . . . Well, goodbye, Prince.

SHUISKY

Goodbye, brother, see you soon.

He shows Pushkin out.

THE TSAR'S PALACE
The tsarevich, drawing a geographical map.
The tsarevna Xenia and her old nurse.

XENIA (*kissing a portrait*)

My dear bridegroom, my splendid prince, it is not I, your
bride, who have you—but a dark grave in a foreign land. I
will never be comforted, I will weep over you eternally.

NURSE

Eh, Tsarevna! For a girl like you, tears are morning
dew; the sun rises, the dew dries up. You'll have another
bridegroom, just as fine and kindly. You'll love him,
my precious child, and forget your prince.

XENIA

No, dear nurse, I'll be faithful to him unto death.

Boris enters.

TSAR

What is it, Xenia? What is it, my dear?
A bride and already a widow in mourning?

You go on weeping over a dead bridegroom.
My child! Fate did not decree that I
Should be the begetter of your felicity.
It may be that I somehow angered heaven,
I was unable to arrange your happiness.
Why is it that you suffer guiltlessly?
—And what are you busy with, my son? What is it?

FYODOR

A plan of Moscow's territory; our kingdom
From end to end. See: here is Moscow,
Here is Novgorod, here is Astrakhan.
Here is the sea, here are the dense forests
Of Perm, and here is Siberia.

TSAR
                                        And what is this
Meandering tracery here?

FYODOR
                              That is the Volga.

TSAR

How good! This is the sweet fruit of study!
You can observe the whole realm at once,
As from a cloud: borders, towns, rivers.
Study, my son: learning condenses for us
The experience of swiftly flowing life.
Someday—and soon, perhaps—all these regions
That you now draw so cleverly on paper
Will come under your hand. Study, my son,
And you will grasp the work of governing
With more ease and clarity.

Semyon Godunov enters.

Look, Godunov's coming to me with a report.
(*to Xenia*)
My dear heart, go to your room upstairs;
Goodbye, my sweet. May God comfort you.

Xenia exits with her nurse.

What is the word, Semyon Nikitich?

SEMYON GODUNOV
Today,
With the first light, Prince Vassily's butler
And Pushkin's servant came with information.

TSAR
Well?

SEMYON GODUNOV
First Pushkin's servant reported
That yesterday morning a messenger from Kraków
Came to their house—and an hour later
Was sent away again without a message.

TSAR
Seize the messenger.

SEMYON GODUNOV
People have been sent already.

TSAR

What about Shuisky?

SEMYON GODUNOV
                    Yesterday he entertained
His friends, the two Miloslavskys, the Buturlins,
Mikhailo Saltykov, Pushkin, and some others;
And they broke up rather late. Only Pushkin
Stayed behind with the host
And went on talking with him for a long time.

TSAR

Send for Shuisky at once.

SEMYON GODUNOV
                    Sire,
He is already here.

TSAR
                    Go bring him in.

Godunov exits.

Contacts with Lithuania! meaning what? . . .
These rebellious Pushkins are offensive to me,
And Shuisky also isn't to be trusted:
He's elusive, but bold and devious . . .

Shuisky enters.

Prince, I need to have a talk with you,
But it seems that you yourself have come on business,
And first I want to hear what you will say.

SHUISKY

Yes, sire: my duty is to tell you
Some very important news.

TSAR

Well, I am listening.

SHUISKY
(softly, pointing to Fyodor)

But, sire . . .

TSAR

The tsarevich may know
What Prince Shuisky knows. Speak openly.

SHUISKY

Tsar, there's news from Lithuania.

TSAR

The same
That the messenger brought to Pushkin yesterday.

SHUISKY

He knows everything! —I thought, sire,
That you might not have learned this secret yet.

TSAR

Never mind, Prince: I want to compare the news;
Otherwise we will never know the truth.

SHUISKY

The only thing I know
Is that an impostor has turned up in Kraków
And that the king and his court favor him.

TSAR

And what's the talk? Who is this impostor?

SHUISKY

I don't know.

TSAR

But . . . how is he dangerous?

SHUISKY

Of course, Tsar: your power is very great,
Your mercy, your zeal and generosity
Have conquered the hearts of your subjects. But you know
The senseless mob is fickle, superstitious,
Rebellious, given easily to futile hopes,
Obedient to the suggestion of the moment,
Deaf and indifferent to the truth,
And it feeds on fables. They like shameless daring.
So if this unknown vagabond should cross
The Lithuanian border, a whole throng
Of madmen will be drawn to him
By the resurrected name of Dimitri.

TSAR

Dimitri! . . .
What? That child? Dimitri! . . . Tsarevich, leave us.

SHUISKY

He's turned all red: there'll be a storm! . . .

FYODOR

Sire,
Allow me to . . .

TSAR

No, my son, go now.

Fyodor exits.

Dimitri's name! . . .

SHUISKY
So he knew nothing.

TSAR
                              Listen, Prince:
Effective measures must be taken at once;
Set up barriers on the Lithuanian border,
So that not one soul can cross into Russia;
So that a hare can't sneak to us from Poland,
Or a raven come flying here from Kraków. Go.

SHUISKY
I'm going.

TSAR
              Wait. This is curious news,
Is it not? Have you ever heard
Of a dead man leaving his coffin and going to question
A tsar, a legitimate tsar, appointed and chosen
By the people, and crowned by a great patriarch?
Laughable? Eh? What? Why aren't you laughing?

SHUISKY
Me, sire?

TSAR
Listen, Prince Vassily:
When I learned that this youth was . . .
That this youth had somehow lost his life,
I sent you to investigate; so now

I adjure you by the cross and in God's name,
In all conscience declare the truth to me:
Did you recognize the murdered child,
And was there not a substitution? Answer.

SHUISKY

I swear to you . . .

TSAR

No, Shuisky, do not swear,
But answer: was it the tsarevich?

SHUISKY

Yes, it was.

TSAR

Think about it, Prince. I promise mercy.
I will not punish a past lie with useless disgrace.
But if you are being devious now, I swear
By my son's head, such evil will befall you,
Such punishment, that the tsar Ivan Vasilyevich
Will shudder with horror in his grave.

SHUISKY

I don't fear punishment; I fear your wrath;
How would I dare deceive you to your face?
And could I be so blindly mistaken
As not to recognize Dimitri? For three days
I visited his body in the cathedral,
Where the people of Uglich brought him. Around him lay
Thirteen corpses torn apart by the crowd,
And on them the signs of decay already showed,
But the tsarevich's childish face was clear

And fresh and calm, as if he were asleep;
The deep wound had not closed, and yet the features
Of his face were unchanged. No, sire,
There is no doubt: Dimitri is laid to rest
In the grave.

TSAR
(calmly)

Enough; go now.

Shuisky exits.

Ohh, that was hard! . . . let me catch my breath . . .
I felt my blood all rush up to my face
And sink down heavily again . . . So that is why
For thirteen years on end the murdered child
Has come to me in dreams! Yes, yes—that's it!
Now I understand. But who is he,
My terrible enemy? Who is so against me?
An empty name, a shadow—can a shadow
Strip me of the purple? Or a sound
Deprive my children of their inheritance?
I must be mad! What am I afraid of?
Blow at this phantom—and it is no more.
So it's decided: I will show no fear—
But I must not let anything go unnoticed . . .
Oh, you are heavy, crown of Monomakh!

KRAKÓW. VISHNEVETSKY'S HOUSE.
The Impostor and Pater Chernikovsky

IMPOSTOR

No, my Father, there will be no hindrance.
I know the spirit of my people; their piety
Is not frenzied: for them the tsar's example
Is sacred. Besides, tolerance is always indifferent.
I'll wager that before two years have passed
My whole people, the whole northern Church,
Will acknowledge the power of St. Peter's vicar.

PATER

May St. Ignatius be your intercessor
When other times come. But meanwhile, Tsarevich,
Hide the seeds of heavenly grace in your soul.
Spiritual duty sometimes orders us
To show a false face to the rest of the world;
Your words and your deeds are judged by people,
But your intentions are seen by God alone.

IMPOSTOR

Amen. Who's there?

A servant enters.

                     Tell them we're receiving.

The doors open; a crowd of Russians and Poles enters.

Comrades! We will be setting out from Kraków
Tomorrow. I will stop over for three days
At your place in Sambor, Mnishek. I know:
Your hospitable castle is distinguished
By its noble magnificence, and is famous for
Its young hostess. I do hope to see
The fair Marina there. And you, my friends,
Lithuanians and Russians, you who raised
Brotherly banners against the common foe,
Against my perfidious enemy, sons of the Slavs,
I will soon lead your dreaded troops
To the much-desired battle. —But I see
New faces among us.

GAVRILA PUSHKIN

              They've come to ask your lordship
To serve you with their swords.

IMPOSTOR

                You're welcome, lads.
Come closer, friends. —But tell me, Pushkin, who
Is this handsome fellow?

PUSHKIN
Prince Kurbsky.

IMPOSTOR

A famous name.
(to Kurbsky)
Are you related to the hero of Kazan?

KURBSKY
I'm his son.

IMPOSTOR
Is he still alive?

KURBSKY
No, he died.

IMPOSTOR
A great mind! A man of war and counsel!
But since the time when, in bitter vengeance
For the wrongs done him, he came with Lithuanians
To Olga's ancient city, all talk of him ceased.

KURBSKY
My father spent the rest of his life in Volyn,
On the estates granted him by Batory.
Alone and quiet, he sought consolation
In studies; but peaceful work gave him no comfort.
He never forgot the fatherland of his youth,
And to the very end he pined for it.

IMPOSTOR

Unhappy leader! How brightly shone the rise
Of his clamorous, stormy life. I rejoice
That through you, a highborn knight, his blood
Can make peace with the fatherland.
The guilt of the fathers should not be remembered;
Peace be to their graves! Come here, Kurbsky.
Your hand! —Is it not strange? The son of Kurbsky
Leads to the throne, whom? Yes—Ioann's son . . .
All is now for me: both people and fate.
—And who are you?

A POLE

Sobansky, a free Polish nobleman.

IMPOSTOR

Praise and honor to you, the child of freedom!
Give him a third of his salary in advance.
—But who are these? I recognize on them
The garments of my native land. They're ours.

KHRUSHCHOV
(bowing low)

Yes, sire, our father. We are your zealous,
Persecuted servants. Fallen into disgrace,
We fled from Moscow to you, to our tsar—
And for you we're ready to lay down our heads,
So that our corpses may become the steps
By which you mount the tsar's throne.

IMPOSTOR
                                        Take heart,
Guiltless martyrs, wait till I get to Moscow,
Then Boris will pay for everything. Who are you?

KARELA

A Cossack. Sent to you from the Don,
From the free army, the brave atamans,
From the upper and lower Cossack ranks,
To look into your bright tsar's eyes
And convey to you the bowing of their heads.

IMPOSTOR

I knew some Don Cossacks. I never doubted
That I would see Cossack bunchuks in my ranks.
We warmly thank our Don forces. We know
That nowadays the Cossacks are unfairly
Oppressed and persecuted; but if God helps us
To mount the throne of our fathers, we will grant them,
As in olden times, our free and faithful Don.

POET
(approaches, makes a low bow, and seizes the skirt of Grishka's coat)
Great Prince, Most Serene Tsarevich!

IMPOSTOR

What do you want?

POET
(hands him a sheet of paper)
Graciously accept
This poor fruit of my painstaking toil.

IMPOSTOR

What is this I see? Latin verses!
A hundredfold sacred is the union of sword and lyre,
One branch of laurel binds the two together.
I was born under the northern sky,

But I know the voice of the Latin muse,
And I love the flowers of Parnassus.
I believe in the prophecies of poets.
No, it is not for nothing that rapture boils
In their ardent breasts: blessed is the deed
That they have glorified beforehand!
Come closer, friend. To remember me,
Accept this gift.

He gives him a signet ring.

       When the behest of fate is accomplished,
When I put on the ancestral crown, I hope
To hear your sweet voice, your inspired hymn again.
Musa gloriam coronat, gloriaque musam.[*]
And so, my friends, goodbye, until tomorrow.

ALL

March on, march on! Long live Dimitri,
Long live the great prince of Moscow!

* The muse crowns glory, glory crowns the muse [Latin].

THE CASTLE OF THE VOEVODA
MNISHEK IN SAMBOR
A suite of brightly lit rooms. Music.
Vishnevetsky, Mnishek

MNISHEK

He only wants to talk with my Marina,
Marina is the only one who interests him . . .
The matter looks terribly like a wedding. Well—
Confess, Vishnevetsky, did you ever think
That my daughter would become a tsaritsa? eh?

VISHNEVETSKY

Yes, it's a wonder . . . and you, Mnishek,
Did you think my servant would mount the Moscow throne?

MNISHEK

And, tell me, what do you make of my Marina?
I only dropped a word to her: Watch out!
Don't let Dimitri slip! . . . and see,
It's all decided. He's caught in her net.

Polish dance music plays. The Impostor and Marina form the first couple.

MARINA
(softly to Dimitri)

So tomorrow evening, at eleven,
In the linden alley by the fountain.

They separate. Another couple.

CAVALIER

What does Dimitri find in her?

LADY
                        Why!

She's a beauty.

CAVALIER
              Yes, a marble nymph:

No life in her eyes and no smile on her lips . . .

A new couple.

LADY

He's not handsome, but he has pleasant looks,
And the tsar's race can be seen in him.

Another couple.

LADY

When do you set out?

CAVALIER

Whenever the tsarevich orders,
We're ready; but it seems that Miss Mnishek
Will keep us as captives with Dimitri.

LADY

A pleasant captivity.

CAVALIER

Of course, if you . . .

They separate. The rooms are empty.

MNISHEK

We old men do not dance anymore,
The noise of music no longer calls to us,
We don't press and kiss those lovely hands—
Oh, I have not forgotten those old antics!
Now it's not the same as it once was:
Young men, truth to tell, are not so bold
And beauty is no longer so lighthearted.
Confess, my friend: it's all grown rather stale.
Let us leave them; let us go, comrade,
And order them to unearth an age-old bottle
Of Hungarian wine, overgrown with moss,
Sit in some corner, the two of us, and sip
The fragrant, flowing liquid, thick as oil,
And meanwhile chat about one thing or another.
Let's go, brother.

VISHNEVETSKY

Agreed, my friend, let's go.

NIGHT. A GARDEN. A FOUNTAIN.

IMPOSTOR
(enters)

Here is the fountain; this is where she'll come.
It seems I wasn't born a coward;
I have seen death up close, and facing death
My soul did not tremble. They threatened me
With eternal captivity, they pursued me—
I did not lose heart and boldly evaded capture.
What is it that now makes me gasp for breath?
What does this irrepressible trembling mean?
Is it the shudder of suppressed desires?
No—it's fear. All day I've been awaiting
The secret meeting with Marina,
Thinking over what I would say to her,
How I would seduce her arrogant mind,
How I would call her the Moscow tsaritsa.
But the hour has come—and I remember nothing.
I cannot find the speeches I rehearsed;
Love confuses my imagination . . .

Ah, something suddenly flashed . . . rustling . . . stillness . . .
No, it's the light of the deceitful moon,
And the whispering of a breeze.

MARINA
(enters)
Tsarevich!

IMPOSTOR
It's her! . . . The blood has frozen in my veins.

MARINA
Dimitri! Is that you?

IMPOSTOR
Sweet, magical voice!

He approaches her.

It's you at last? Do I see you here with me
Alone, under the quiet cover of night?
How slowly the dull day passed! How slowly
The setting sun faded! How long I spent
Waiting for you here in the evening darkness!

MARINA
The hours race by, and time is dear to me—
I did not arrange to meet you here
To listen to a lover's tender talk.
Words aren't needed. I believe you love me;
But listen: I'm resolved to join my destiny
With yours, stormy and uncertain as it is,
And I have the right to demand one thing of you,

Dimitri: I demand that you reveal to me
Your soul's secret hopes, intentions, even fears;
So that boldly, hand in hand with you, I may
Set out in life—not with a child's blindness,
Not as the slave of a husband's merest whim,
Your silent concubine—but as your worthy spouse,
As the helpmeet of the tsar of Moscow.

IMPOSTOR

Oh, for one little hour let me forget
The cares and worries of my fate! And you yourself,
Forget that the one you see before you is
The tsarevich. Marina! you behold in me
A lover, the one that you have chosen,
Who is happy for a single glance from you.
Oh, listen to the pleadings of my love,
Let me speak out all that fills my heart.

MARINA

Not now, Prince. You tarry—and meanwhile
The devotion of your henchmen is cooling off,
Your dangers and your difficulties grow
More dangerous and difficult by the hour.
Doubtful rumors already fly around,
Novelty already replaces novelty;
And Godunov is making his arrangements . . .

IMPOSTOR

What is Godunov? Is your love,
Which is my only bliss, in Boris's power?
No, no. I now look with indifference

At his throne, at his sovereign power.
Your love . . . what is my life without it,
And the splendor of glory, and the Russian scepter?
In the remote steppe, in a poor hut—you,
You will replace the tsar's crown for me,
Your love . . .

MARINA

That is shameful; don't forget
Your lofty, sacred mission: your rank should be
Dearer to you than all joys, all enticements
Of life; you cannot put it on a par
With anything. Know: it is not to an ardent youth
Insanely captivated by my beauty
That I solemnly give my hand, but to the heir
Of Moscow's throne, to the tsarevich,
The man who has been spared by fate.

IMPOSTOR

Don't torment me, beautiful Marina,
Don't say it is my rank and not myself
That you have chosen. Marina! you don't know
How painfully you wound my heart that way—
What if . . . oh, terrible doubt! Tell me:
If blind fate had not appointed me
To be born tsarevich, were I not Ioann's son,
That youth long forgotten by the world—
Would you . . . would you love me then? . . .

MARINA

You are Dimitri and you can be no one else;
I cannot love another man.

IMPOSTOR
No! enough:
I do not want to share with a dead man
The beloved woman who belongs to him.
No, enough pretending! I will tell you
The whole truth; know then: your Dimitri
Is long dead and buried, and will not rise.
And you want to know who I am? Very well,
I'll tell you: I am a poor monk.
Bored by monastic seclusion, under the cowl
I nurtured my bold plan, preparing to offer
The world a miracle—and finally I fled
From my cell to the Cossacks,
To their riotous camps, where I learned to master
Horse and sword; and then I came to your parts,
Called myself Dimitri, and so deceived
The brainless Poles. Well, what do you say,
Haughty Marina, are you pleased with my confession?
Why are you silent?

MARINA
Oh, shame! Oh, misery!

Silence.

IMPOSTOR
(*aside*)
How far this angry outburst has misled me!
The happiness attained with so much effort
I may have ruined forever. What have I done,
Madman?

(*aloud*)

> I see, I see: You are ashamed
> To be loved by a man who is not a prince.
> Then speak the fatal word;
> My destiny is in your hands now. Decide:
> I'm waiting.

He falls on his knees.

MARINA

> Stand up, wretched impostor.
> Do you imagine that by kneeling down
> You can move my ambitious heart, as if
> I were a weak and credulous little girl?
> You are mistaken, friend,
> I have seen knights and noble counts at my feet,
> But I coldly rejected their entreaties,
> Not just so that some poor runaway monk . . .

IMPOSTOR

> Don't scorn the young impostor; perhaps in him
> A valor is concealed that makes him worthy
> Of the Moscow throne, worthy of your priceless hand . . .

MARINA

> Worthy of a disgraceful noose, you brazen man!

IMPOSTOR

> I am guilty; overcome by pride
> I deceived God and tsars, I lied to the world;
> But you ought not to punish me, Marina;
> I'm in the right before you. I could not deceive you.

For me you were the only sacred being,
I did not dare pretend before you. Love,
Jealous, blind love alone forced me
To tell you all.

MARINA
What's there to boast of, madman!
Who ever demanded a confession from you?
If you, a nameless vagabond, by some miracle,
Could blind two nations, you should at least have proved
Worthy of success and secured your bold deceit
By persistent, deep, eternal secrecy.
Tell me, how can I surrender myself,
How, forgetting my family and a maiden's modesty,
Can I unite my destiny with yours,
When you yourself so simply, so lightheartedly
Expose your shame? He just babbles away
Out of love for me! I wonder why you haven't
Revealed yourself before now to my father
Out of friendship, to our king out of good cheer,
Or to Vishnevetsky out of servile zeal.

IMPOSTOR
I swear to you that you alone could draw
This confession from me. I swear to you
That never, anywhere, not at a feast
Over a reckless cup, nor in secret, friendly talk,
Nor under the threat of a knife or painful torture
Would my tongue betray this heavy secret.

MARINA

You swear! and so I must believe you—
Oh, I do believe you—but may I know
What you swear by? Is it the name of God,
As a pious foster child of the Jesuits?
Or by your honor as a noble knight,
Or maybe it's just by one sovereign word,
As a tsar's son? Is that it? Speak.

DIMITRI
(proudly)

The shade of Ivan the Terrible adopted me,
Dimitri he proclaimed me from the grave,
Stirred up the nations around me, and appointed
Boris my victim—I am the tsarevich.
Enough, I find it shameful
To stoop before a haughty Polish wench.
Farewell forever. The game of bloody war,
The vast cares of my destiny will, I hope,
Stifle the sorrow of my love. Oh, how I'll hate you,
When the ardor of shameful passion is behind me!
I go now—either death or the crown awaits
My head in Russia, but whether I find the death
Of a warrior in honest combat, or a villain
On a public scaffold, you will not be my soulmate,
You will not share my destiny with me.
But it may be that you will regret the lot
You have rejected.

MARINA

And what if I should hasten
To expose your bold deceit before the world?

IMPOSTOR

Do you fancy I'm afraid of you?
That they will sooner believe a Polish girl
Than a Russian tsarevich? —But know this,
That neither king nor pope nor courtiers
Think about the truthfulness of my words.
Whether I'm Dimitri or not—what do they care?
But I am a good pretext for strife and war.
That's all they need, and you, rebellious girl,
Believe me, they'll keep you quiet! So, farewell.

MARINA

Wait, Tsarevich. At last I hear the voice
Not of a boy, but of a man. It reconciles me
With you, Prince, I forget your mad impulse
And see Dimitri again. But listen: it's time,
It's time, wake up, don't tarry any longer;
Lead the regiments quickly to Moscow—
Purge the Kremlin, mount the Moscow throne,
Then send an ambassador to ask for me.
But, God is my witness, until your foot
Marches up the steps to the throne, until
You depose Godunov, I'll hear no talk of love.

She exits.

IMPOSTOR

No—it's easier to fight with Godunov
Or quibble with a Jesuit at the court

Than with a woman—devil take them; I can't.
She twists, she twines, she meanders,
She slips through my fingers, hisses, threatens, stings.
A snake! a snake! I had good reason to tremble.
She nearly did me in. But it's decided:
In the morning I will set out with the army.

THE LITHUANIAN BORDER

The year 1604, the sixteenth of October
Prince Kurbsky and the Impostor, both on horseback.
The troops are approaching the border.

KURBSKY
(arriving first)

Here, here it is! Here is the Russian border!
Holy Russia, Fatherland! I am yours!
I scornfully shake the dust of a foreign land
From my clothes—I greedily drink in new air:
It is my own! . . . Now your soul, O my father,
Will be comforted, and in their grave
Your exiled bones will rejoice! It flashes again,
This our ancestral sword, this glorious sword,
The terror of dark Kazan, this trusty sword,
The servant of Moscow's tsars! It will feast now,
Wielded for its trusty sovereign! . . .

IMPOSTOR
(riding slowly, with hanging head)

How happy he is! How his pure soul rises

With joy and glory! O my knight, I envy you.
The son of Kurbsky, brought up in exile,
Forgetting the offenses suffered by his father,
Atoning for his guilt after his death,
You prepare to shed your blood for Ivan's son;
To restore the lawful tsar to your fatherland . . .
You're right, your soul should be aflame with joy.

KURBSKY

Aren't you, too, rejoicing in your soul?
Here is our Russia: it is yours, Tsarevich.
There your people's hearts are waiting for you;
Your Moscow, your Kremlin, your scepter.

IMPOSTOR

Oh, Kurbsky, Russian blood is going to flow!
You have raised your sword for the tsar, you're clean.
But I am leading you against your brothers;
I've summoned Lithuania to Russia, I am showing
The enemy the secret road to my fair Moscow! . . .
But let my sin fall not upon me,
But on you, Boris, you, the regicide!
—Forward!

KURBSKY

Forward! and woe to Godunov!

They gallop off. The troops cross the border.

THE TSAR'S COUNCIL
The Tsar, the Patriarch, and Boyars

TSAR

Can it be? Some fugitive defrocked monk
Is leading the enemy's troops against us,
And dares to write and threaten us? Enough,
It's time to subdue the madman! —Go, Trubetskoy,
And you, Basmanov: my diligent commanders
Need help. The rebel has besieged Chernigov.
Save the city and its citizens.

BASMANOV
Sire,
Before three months are out, all this talk
Of the impostor will cease; we will bring him to Moscow
In an iron cage like an exotic beast.
I swear to God.

He exits with Trubetskoy.

TSAR

The Swedish king
Has sent me ambassadors offering an alliance;
But we do not need any foreign aid;
Our own people are enough for making war
And fending off the traitor and the Poles.
I refused.

Shchelkalov! Send out orders
To commanders in every corner to mount up
And send the people to serve as in the old days;
Recruit from the monasteries as well.
In former times, when the fatherland faced trouble,
Even hermits went to fight. But we don't wish
To trouble them now; let them pray for us—
Such is the tsar's order, sealed by the boyars.
Now we must resolve an important question:
You know that the impudent impostor
Has spread perfidious rumors everywhere;
Everywhere the letters he has sent
Have sown anxiety and doubt;
There's rebellious whispering in the public squares,
Minds are boiling . . . they must be cooled down;
I would like to forestall executions,
But with what and how? Let us decide. You first,
Holy Father, reveal your thoughts to us.

PATRIARCH

Blessed be the Almighty, who instills
The spirit of mercy and meek patience in your soul,
Great sovereign; you do not wish to destroy

The sinner, you quietly wait till the error passes:
It will pass, and the sun of eternal truth
Will shine upon all.

                         Your faithful churchman,
Who is no wise judge in earthly matters,
Makes bold to let his voice be heard today.
    The devil's son, the cursed former monk,
Cunningly passed for Dimitri among the people;
He clothed himself with the tsarevich's name,
As with a stolen garment: but once this garment
Is torn off, his own nakedness will shame him.
    God himself sends us the means to do it:
Know, sire, that six years ago,
The same year the Lord blessed you to take up
The scepter, one evening a certain simple shepherd,
Already a venerable old man, came to me
And told me a wondrous secret.
"In my young years," he said, "I became blind
And after that could not tell night from day
Till my old age: in vain I tried to treat it
With medicines and magic spells; in vain
I went to venerate great miracle workers
In monasteries; in vain I sprinkled
My darkened eyes with the healing waters
Of holy springs; the Lord would send no cure.
In the end I lost all hope, became accustomed
To my darkness, and even in my dreams
I did not see the things I had seen before,
But dreamed only of sounds. Once, fast asleep,
I heard a child's voice say: 'Get up, Grandpa,
Go to the town of Uglich, to the cathedral

Of the Transfiguration, and pray there
Over my little grave. God is merciful—
And I will forgive you.' 'But who are you?'
I asked the child's voice. 'The tsarevich Dimitri.
The King of Heaven took me into the host
Of His angels, and now I am a great miracle worker!
Go, old man.' I woke up and thought:
Well, so? Maybe God will really grant me
A belated cure. I'll go. And I set out
On the long journey. I reached Uglich, I went
To the holy cathedral and heard the liturgy,
My zealous soul was all afire, I wept
So sweetly, as if the blindness were pouring out
Of my eyes at the same time as the tears.
When people started leaving, I turned to my grandson
And said: 'Ivan, take me to the grave
Of the tsarevich Dimitri.' The boy led me there—
And as I quietly prayed before the grave,
My eyes were opened, and I saw God's world,
And my grandson, and the tomb."
That, sire, is what the old man told me.

General confusion. During this speech, Boris wipes his face
several times with his handkerchief.

I then sent a messenger to Uglich
And learned that many sufferers had received
A similar recovery at the tsarevich's tomb.
    Here's my advice: order the holy relics
Transferred to the Kremlin and have them placed
In the Archangel Cathedral; then the people

Will see clearly the deceit of the godless villain,
And the demons' power will vanish like dust.

Silence.

PRINCE SHUISKY

Holy Father, who can know the ways
Of the Almighty? It's not for me to judge.
He can endow the infant's remains
With incorrupt sleep and wonder-working power,
But the popular rumors need to be examined
Diligently and without prejudice;
And can we give a thought to such great things
In these stormy and tumultuous times?
Won't it be said that we are brazenly making
Holy relics a weapon in worldly matters?
The people even now are on the brink of madness,
And even now there is enough loud talk:
It's not the time to stir up people's minds
With unexpected though important novelties.
I see myself it's necessary to destroy
The rumor sown by this defrocked renegade;
But there are other—simpler—means for that.
So, sire—whenever it pleases you,
I myself will appear on the people's square,
Reason with their madness, shame them for it,
And reveal the wicked vagabond's deceit.

TSAR

So be it! Most holy patriarch,
I ask you to kindly come to my chambers:
I shall have need of your counsel presently.

He exits. The boyars all go with him.

ONE BOYAR
(quietly to another)

Did you notice how our sovereign went pale
And big drops of sweat ran down his face?

ANOTHER

I confess, I didn't dare to raise my eyes,
Or draw a breath, or even make a move.

FIRST

Prince Shuisky saved the day. And good for him!

A PLAIN NEAR NOVGOROD-SEVERSKY
The year 1604, the twenty-first of December
Battle

SOLDIERS

(fleeing in disorder)

Trouble, trouble! The tsarevich! The Poles! There they are!
There they are!

Enter Captains Margeret and Walter Rozen.

MARGERET

Where going, where going? Allons . . . aboot face!

A FLEEING MAN

Aboot face yourself, if you want, you damned heathen.

MARGERET

Quoi? quoi?

ANOTHER

Quack, quack, you foreign duck, if you like quacking at the
Russian tsarevich; but we're Orthodox people.

MARGERET

Qu'est-ce à dire Orphotoxe? . . . Sacrés gueux, maudites
canailles! Mordieu, mein herr, j'enrage: on dirait que ça n'a
pas des bras pour frapper, ça n'a que des jambes pour foutre
le camp.*

W. ROZEN

Es ist Schande.†

MARGERET

Ventre-saint-gris! Je ne bouge plus d'un pas—puisque le
vin est tiré, il faut le boire. Qu'en dites-vous, mein herr?‡

W. ROZEN

Sie haben Recht.§

MARGERET

Tudieu, il y fait chaud! Ce diable d'Imposteur, comme
ils l'appellent, est un bougre qui a du poil au cul. Qu'en
pensez-vous, mein herr?**

W. ROZEN

Oh, ja!

---

* What does Orphotoxe mean? Miserable wretches, cursed trash! Zounds, *mein
herr*, I'm furious: you'd say it has no arms to strike with, it only has legs to run
away with.
† It's a disgrace.
‡ Gadzooks! I won't take another step—since the wine is poured, it must be
drunk. What do you say, *mein herr*?
§ You're right.
** Goddamn, it's hot going! This devil of an impostor, as they call him, is a
bugger with a wild hair up his ass. What do you think, *mein herr*?

MARGERET

Hé! voyez donc, voyez donc! L'action s'engage sur
les derrières de l'ennemi. Ce doit être le brave Basmanoff,
qui aurait fait une sortie.[*]

W. ROZEN

Ich glaube das.[†]

Enter Germans.

MARGERET

Ha, ha! voici nos allemands. Messieurs! . . . Mein herr,
dites leur donc de se rallier et, sacrebleu, chargeons![‡]

W. ROZEN

Sehr gut. Halt![§]

The Germans line up.

Marsch!

GERMANS

Hilf Gott![**]

They fight. The Russians flee again.

---

[*] Hey, look at that, look at that! Action has begun on the enemy's rear. It must
be brave Basmanov has made a sortie.
[†] I think so.
[‡] Aha! here are our Germans. Gentlemen! . . . *Mein herr*, tell them to join in and,
by God, we'll charge!
[§] Very good. Halt!
[**] God be with us!

THE POLES

Victory! Victory! Glory to Tsar Dimitri!

DIMITRI
(on horseback)

Sound the halt! We are victorious. Enough: spare the
Russian blood. Halt!

Drums and trumpets.

CATHEDRAL SQUARE IN MOSCOW
People

ONE

Will the tsar leave the cathedral soon?

ANOTHER

The liturgy's over; now it's a prayer service.

THE ONE

Well, so? Did they already curse *that one*?

THE OTHER

I stood on the porch and heard the deacon shout: Grishka
Otrepyev—anathema!

THE ONE

Let them curse their fill; the tsarevich couldn't care less
about Otrepyev.

THE OTHER

Now they're singing "Memory Eternal" to the tsarevich.

THE ONE

"Memory Eternal" to a living person! They're going to
get it for this godlessness.

A THIRD

Shh! There's noise. Maybe it's the tsar?

A FOURTH

No, it's the holy fool.

The holy fool enters in an iron hat, hung all over with chains,
surrounded by street urchins.

URCHINS

Nikolka, Nikolka—iron hat! *Nya-nya-nya-a-a* . . .

OLD WOMAN

Leave the blessed man alone, you devils. —Nikolka, pray
for me, a sinner.

HOLY FOOL

Gimme, gimme, gimme a little kopeck.

OLD WOMAN

Here's a little kopeck for you; remember me in your prayers.

HOLY FOOL
               (*sits down on the ground and sings*)
The moon is shining,
The puppy's whining,
Holy fool, get up,
And pray to God!

The boys surround him again.

ONE OF THEM

Hello there, Nikolka; why don't you take your hat off?
(*Gives him a flick on his iron hat*) Makes a nice clink!

HOLY FOOL

I've got a little kopeck.

BOY

Not true! Show me!

He snatches the kopeck and runs away.

HOLY FOOL
(*weeps*)
He made off with my little kopeck; he's offended Nikolka!

PEOPLE

The tsar, the tsar is coming!

The tsar comes out of the cathedral. A boyar walks ahead of him, distributing alms. More boyars.

HOLY FOOL

Boris, Boris! The children offended Nikolka . . .

TSAR

Give him alms. Why is he crying?

HOLY FOOL

The little children offended Nikolka . . . Order them killed, the way you killed the little tsarevich.

BOYARS

Out of the way, you idiot! Seize the idiot!

TSAR

Let him be. Pray for me, poor Nikolka.

He exits.

HOLY FOOL
(to his back)

No, no! It's wrong to pray for the tsar Herod—the Mother of God forbids it.

THE TOWN OF SEVSK

Impostor, surrounded by his people.

IMPOSTOR

Where is the prisoner?

POLE

Here.

IMPOSTOR

Send him to me.

Enter Russian prisoner.

Who are you?

PRISONER

Rozhnov, a Moscow nobleman.

IMPOSTOR

Have you been serving long?

PRISONER

Nearly a month.

IMPOSTOR

Are you not ashamed, Rozhnov, that you have raised
Your sword against me?

PRISONER

What else could I do?

It was on orders.

IMPOSTOR

Did you fight at Seversky?

PRISONER

I came from Moscow two weeks after the battle.

IMPOSTOR

How is Godunov?

PRISONER

He was very alarmed
By the lost battle and the wounding of Mstislavsky,
And he sent Shuisky to take command of the army.

IMPOSTOR

Why did he call Basmanov back to Moscow?

PRISONER

The tsar rewarded his services with honor
And with gold. Basmanov is now sitting
In the tsar's Council.

IMPOSTOR

He was more needed in the army.

Well, how are things in Moscow?

PRISONER

All quiet, thank God.

IMPOSTOR

What? Waiting for me?

PRISONER

God knows. These days
Few are bold enough to talk of you.
This one would have his tongue cut off,
That one his head—and so it really goes!
Another day, another execution.
The prisons are packed. Three men get together
On a square—lo and behold, a spy
Is hanging around, and the sovereign himself
Interrogates the informers at his leisure.
Nothing but trouble; better to keep quiet.

IMPOSTOR

An enviable life Boris's people lead!
Well, what about the army?

PRISONER

What about it?
Clothed, fed, content with everything.

IMPOSTOR

How many are they?

PRISONER

God knows.

IMPOSTOR

Some thirty thousand?

PRISONER

Maybe as much as fifty thousand in all.

The Impostor ponders. Those around him exchange glances.

IMPOSTOR

Well! What's the talk about me in your camp?

PRISONER

What they say about your honor
(No offense intended) is that you're a thief,
But a fine fellow.

IMPOSTOR
(laughing)
And I'll prove it to them
By my acts: friends, we won't wait for Shuisky:
I congratulate you: tomorrow is the battle.

He exits.

ALL

Long live Dimitri!

A POLE
Tomorrow is the battle!
They have some fifty thousand, and we have barely
Fifteen. He's lost his mind.

ANOTHER
It's nothing, friend:
One Pole can challenge five hundred Muscovites.

PRISONER

Oh yes, you can. But when it comes to fighting,
You'll run away from one, you empty windbag.

POLE

If you had a sword on you, you brazen prisoner,
This (*points to his sword*) would be enough to humble you.

PRISONER

We Russians can get along without a sword:
How would you like this (*shows his fist*), you harebrained fool!

The Pole gives him a proud look and silently walks away.
Everyone laughs.

FOREST
False Dimitri, Pushkin
A dying horse lies some distance away.

FALSE DIMITRI
My poor horse! How briskly he galloped
Into his last battle today, and, already wounded,
How swiftly he carried me—my poor horse!

PUSHKIN
(to himself)
Just see what he pities! His horse! When our whole army
Has been ground to dust!

IMPOSTOR
Listen, it may be
That he's just tired from his wound and needs to rest.

PUSHKIN
Not a chance; he's dying.

IMPOSTOR

(goes to his horse)

My poor horse! . . .
What can we do? Take the bridle off,
Unfasten the saddle girth, let him die
In freedom.

He unbridles and unsaddles the horse. Several Poles enter.

Ah, greetings, gentlemen!
Why do I not see Kurbsky in your midst?
I saw him ride today into the thick of battle;
Hundreds of swords rose up over the hero
Like waving wheat, but his sword rose still higher,
And his battle cry was louder than the rest.
Where is my hero?

A POLE

Lying on the field of death.

IMPOSTOR

Honor to the brave man and peace to his soul!
How few of us survived the battle. Traitors!
Vile Cossacks, curse you, you were our ruin—
Not to fend off even three minutes of an attack!
I'll show them! I'll hang every tenth man of them,
The villains!

PUSHKIN

Well, whoever is to blame,
In any case we're totally destroyed,
Annihilated.

IMPOSTOR

But the game was ours;
I was about to crush the front line; then
The Germans smartly drove us back—fine soldiers!
By God, I like them, I'll definitely form
My guard of honor from their ranks.

PUSHKIN

And where will we spend the night?

IMPOSTOR

Here in the forest. As good a place as any!
We'll set out at dawn, reach Rylsk by dinnertime.
Good night.

He lies down, puts the saddle under his head, and falls asleep.

PUSHKIN

Pleasant dreams, Tsarevich!
Ground to dust, fleeing to save his life,
He is as carefree as a foolish child;
Providence is surely watching over him;
And as for us, my friends, let's not lose heart.

MOSCOW. THE TSAR'S PALACE.

Boris, Basmanov

TSAR

He is defeated, what's the good of that?
We were crowned with victory in vain.
He gathered the dispersed army again
And threatens us from the walls of Putivl'.
What do our heroes do in the meantime?
They camp by Kromy, where a band of Cossacks
Laugh at them from behind the rotten stockade.
That's our glory! No, I'm not pleased with them;
I'm sending you to lead them, naming you
General by brains and not by pedigree;
Let their arrogance pine for their privileges;
It's time we scorned the murmur of the highborn mob
And put an end to this pernicious custom.

BASMANOV

Ah, sire, a hundred times blessed be the day
When the Registers of Nobility and with them
Their strife and arrogance are devoured by fire.

TSAR

That day is not far off; but first
Let me quell the people's agitation.

BASMANOV

Why pay heed to that; the people are always
Secretly given to agitation:
So a fiery steed chews his bit; so a boy rebels
Against his father's power; and what then?
The rider calmly reins in his steed,
And the father overrules his boy.

TSAR

The steed sometimes throws the rider off,
A son does not forever yield outright
To his father's will. Only unrelenting strictness
Can restrain the people. So thought Ioann,
The subduer of storms, the wise autocrat,
And so thought his fierce grandson. No, the people
Are not sensible to mercy: do them good—
They will not thank you; rob and punish them—
You will be no worse off.

A boyar enters.

What is it?

BOYAR

Foreign visitors have been brought in.

TSAR

I'll go and receive them; wait, Basmanov,
Stay here: I must still talk with you.

He exits.

BASMANOV

A lofty, sovereign spirit. God grant he deals
With the cursed Otrepyev, and he will do
Much, much more good for Russia.
In his mind he bears an important thought.
It must not be allowed to simmer down.
What a future opens for me when he breaks
The horn of boyar power! I have no equals
On the battlefield; I'll stand first beside the throne . . .
And maybe . . . maybe . . . But what is this strange noise?

*Alarm. Boyars and palace attendants run about in disorder, meet,
and whisper.*

ONE

Send for a doctor!

ANOTHER

To the patriarch—quickly.

A THIRD

He's calling for the tsarevich, the tsarevich!

A FOURTH

Confessor!

BASMANOV

What's happened?

A FIFTH

The tsar is ill.

A SIXTH

The tsar is dying.

BASMANOV

My God!

THE FIFTH

He sat on his throne and suddenly fell down —
Blood started pouring from his mouth and ears.

The tsar is brought in on a chair; enter the tsar's whole family and all of the boyars.

TSAR

Leave, all of you, let only the tsarevich
Remain with me.

They all exit.

I am dying.
Let us embrace: farewell, my son; you will
Begin your reign now . . . O God, God!
I shall appear before Thee now—and my soul
Has no time to be purified by confession.
But I feel—my son, you are dearer to me
Than my soul's salvation . . . and so be it!
I was born a subject, and it behooved me
To die a subject in obscurity;
But I reached the highest power . . . how?
Don't ask. It's enough that you are innocent,
And you will reign now by right of succession.
I, I alone, will answer to God for all . . .
O my dear son, do not delude yourself,
Do not voluntarily blind yourself—
You are taking power in stormy days:

This bizarre impostor is dangerous,
He has armed himself with a terrible name . . .
Being versed in governing for many years,
I was able to control turmoil and unrest;
They trembled in fear before me; treachery
Did not dare raise its voice. But you, a young,
Inexperienced ruler, how will you
Govern under such storms, quench unrest,
Manacle treason? But God is great!
To youth He gives wisdom, to weakness—strength . . .
Listen: first choose a counselor, someone
Trustworthy, coolheaded, ripe in years,
Loved by the people, and among the boyars
Esteemed for his lineage or his famous deeds—
Say, Shuisky. Then for the army these days
You need a skillful leader: send in Basmanov,
And firmly endure the boyars' grumbling.
From an early age you sat with me in the Duma,
You know all the procedures of state power;
Do not change the course of things. Habit
Is the soul of power. Lately I was forced
To bring back disgraces, executions—you
May abolish them; the people will bless you for it
As they did your uncle when he took the throne
Of Ivan the Terrible. After some time
Gradually tighten the reins of power again.
For now relax them, without letting go . . .
Be merciful, accessible to foreigners,
Accept their service trustingly.
Keep strictly to the Church's precepts; be reticent;
The tsar's voice should not vanish in the air

For nothing; like the ringing of a sacred bell,
It should proclaim only great grief or great festivity.
O my dear son, you're drawing near the age
When a woman's face stirs up a man's blood.
Keep, keep the holy purity
Of innocence and of proud modesty:
One who gets accustomed in his youth
To wallowing in wanton sensual pleasures,
In manhood will turn sullen and bloodthirsty,
And his mind will be prematurely darkened.
In your family always be the head;
Honor your mother, but govern on your own—
You are a man and a tsar; love your sister,
You alone are her protector now.

FYODOR
(on his knees)

No, no—live on and rule for many years:
The people and we will perish without you.

TSAR

It is all over—my eyes have gone dark,
I feel a sepulchral coldness . . .

*Enter the patriarch, bishops, followed by boyars. The tsaritsa is
supported under the arms; the tsarevna is weeping.*

                    Who's there?
Ah! the clergy . . . Yes! the sacred tonsuring . . .
The hour has struck, the tsar becomes a monk—
And the dark coffin will be my cell . . .
Hold off a little, holy patriarch,

I'm still the tsar: pay heed to me, boyars:
Here is the one to whom I entrust the throne;
Swear allegiance to Fyodor . . . Basmanov,
My friends . . . on the verge of the grave I beg you
To serve him with zealousness and truth!
He is still so young and innocent . . .
Do you swear?

BOYARS

We swear.

TSAR

I am content.

Forgive me my temptations and my sins,
And my offenses, voluntary or hidden . . .
Approach, holy Father, I am ready.

The rite of tonsuring begins. The women faint and are carried out.

HEADQUARTERS

Basmanov leads in Pushkin.

BASMANOV

Come in here and speak quite freely.
So it was he himself who sent you to me?

PUSHKIN

He is offering you his friendship
And the first rank below him in the Moscow tsardom.

BASMANOV

But I have already been raised high
By Fyodor. I am commander of the army,
For my sake he ignored the register of nobility
And the wrath of the boyars—to him I swore allegiance.

PUSHKIN

You swore allegiance to the lawful heir
Of the throne; but what if there lives another man
Who is still more lawful? . . .

BASMANOV

                Listen, Pushkin, enough,
Don't talk nonsense; I know who he is.

PUSHKIN

Russia and Lithuania have long recognized him
As Dimitri. I, incidentally, do not insist on it.
He may be the real Dimitri, or he may be
An impostor. I know only that sooner or later
Boris's son will surrender Moscow to him.

BASMANOV

As long as I stand for the youthful tsar,
He will remain on the throne; we have
Enough soldiers, thank God! I will encourage them
With victories. And you, who will you send
Against me? The Cossack Karela or the Pole Mnishek?
You aren't many, only some eight thousand.

PUSHKIN

You're mistaken: we're even less than that—
I'll tell you myself that our army is trash,
That the Cossacks are busy plundering the villages,
The Poles do nothing except boast and drink,
And as for the Russians . . . what can I say . . .
I won't put on any pretenses before you;
But do you know what makes us strong, Basmanov?
Not the army, no, and not the Polish aid,
But sentiment; yes! the people's sentiment.
Do you remember Dimitri's triumph
And his peaceful conquests, when towns obediently
Surrendered to him without a single shot,

And the mob tied up the stubborn chiefs?
You saw yourself how unwillingly your army
Fought him—when was that? It was under Boris!
And now? . . . No, Basmanov, it's too late
To resist, and to fan the war's cold ashes.
For all your mind and firm will, you won't stand;
Isn't it better to be the first to give
A wise example, to proclaim Dimitri
The tsar and make an eternal friend of him?
What do you think?

BASMANOV

You'll find out tomorrow.

PUSHKIN

Be resolute.

BASMANOV

Goodbye.

PUSHKIN

Think well, Basmanov.

He exits.

BASMANOV

He's right, he's right; treason is brewing everywhere.
What shall I do? Wait until the rebels
Bind me and hand me over to Otrepyev?
Wouldn't it be better to forestall
The violent outbreak and . . . But to betray
My oath! To earn dishonor for all the ages!
To repay the trust of the child monarch
With a terrible betrayal . . . It is easy

For a disgraced and banished man to contemplate
Rebellion and conspiracy, but for me,
For me, the favorite of the sovereign . . .
Death . . . power . . . national disaster . . .

He falls to thinking.

Come here! Who's there? (*He whistles.*) My horse!
Sound the muster!

BY THE PLATFORM ON RED SQUARE

Pushkin enters, surrounded by people.

PEOPLE

The tsarevich has sent us this boyar.
Let's listen to what the boyar has to say.
Come here! Come here!

PUSHKIN
(mounts the platform)
Citizens of Moscow,
The tsarevich has asked me to bow to you.

He bows.

You know how the providence of Heaven
Saved the tsarevich from the murderer's hand;
He was on his way to punish the evildoer,
But divine justice already struck Boris down.
Russia has submitted to Dimitri;
Basmanov himself, with zealous repentance,
Had the army swear allegiance, and Dimitri

Is coming to you now with love and peace.
Will you, to please the family of Godunov,
Raise your hand against the lawful tsar,
The descendant of Monomakh?

PEOPLE

No, surely not.

PUSHKIN

Citizens of Moscow! Everybody knows
How much you suffered under the cruel outsider:
Banishments, executions, dishonor, taxes,
And hard work, and famine—you endured it all.
Dimitri intends to bestow favors on you,
Boyars, nobility, clerks, the military,
Merchants, tradesmen—on all honest folk.
You will not be insanely obstinate
And haughtily reject these favors, will you?
He is coming to take the throne of the tsars,
His forefathers—with a dread company.
Fear God and do not anger the tsar.
Swear allegiance to the lawful ruler;
Humble yourselves, immediately send
A metropolitan to Dimitri's camp,
Boyars, clerks, and elected officials,
To bow down before their father and their sovereign.

He steps down. Noise among the people.

PEOPLE

What's there to talk about? The boyar made sense.
Long live Dimitri, long live our father!

A PEASANT FROM THE PLATFORM

People, people! To the Kremlin! To the tsar's palace!
Let us go and tie up Boris's puppy!

PEOPLE
(rushing in a crowd)

Tie him up! Drown him! Long live Dimitri!
Death to the line of Boris Godunov!

THE KREMLIN. BORIS'S HOUSE.
Guards by the porch.
Fyodor is at the window.

A BEGGAR
Alms for the love of Christ!

GUARD
Go away, talking to prisoners is not permitted.

FYODOR
Go away, old man. I'm poorer than you—you're free.

Xenia, her head veiled, also comes to the window.

ONE OF THE PEOPLE
Brother and sister! Poor children, like birds in a cage.

ANOTHER
Why pity them? A cursed breed!

THE ONE
The father was a villain, but the children are innocent.

THE OTHER

The apple never falls far from the tree.

XENIA

Brother, brother, it seems some boyars are coming to us.

FYODOR

It's Golitsyn, Mosalsky. The others I don't know.

XENIA

Ah, brother, my heart is sinking.

Enter Golitsyn, Mosalsky, Molchanov, and Sherefedinov. Three bodyguards follow them.

PEOPLE

Make way, make way. The boyars are coming.

They go into the house.

ONE OF THE PEOPLE

Why are they going in there?

A SECOND

Probably to swear in Fyodor Godunov.

A THIRD

Really? —Listen, what noise there is inside! Commotion, fighting . . .

PEOPLE

Hear that? Shrieking! It's a woman's voice. Let's go in. The door is locked. The shouting has died down.

The door opens. Mosalsky appears on the doorstep.

MOSALSKY

People! Maria Godunov and her son Fyodor have poisoned themselves. We have seen their dead bodies.

The people are mute with horror.

Why are you mute? Shout, "Long live the tsar Dimitri Ivanovich!"

The people are silent.

The End

GLOSSARY

Ataman: A chief military commander in Cossack armies.

Boyar: The boyars were members of the Russian feudal aristocracy and held considerable power until the centralization of authority under Ivan IV (the Terrible) in the sixteenth century.

Bunchuk: A pole topped with a length of tail hair from a horse or yak, which served as a military banner among the nomadic peoples of Eurasia.

Cossacks: Members of Slavic-speaking, semi-independent, democratic Orthodox communities living on the steppes around the basins of the Don and Dnieper Rivers.

Crown of Monomakh: The crown named for the grand duke Vladimir II Monomakh is an elaborate headpiece made of gold, fur, and jewels, which became the first symbolic crown of Russian rulers. Preserved in the Kremlin Armory museum, it dates to the early fourteenth century, though Monomakh reigned over Kievan Rus some two centuries earlier.

Duma: A legislative council of boyars advising the grand dukes in medieval Russia.

Litva, Rus: *Litva* is Russian for Lithuania; Rus was the name of a Norse people who settled between the Baltic and Black Seas, founded the state of Kievan Rus, and eventually gave their name to Russia.

Metropolitan: The archbishop of an Orthodox Church diocese.

Patriarch: In 1589 the bishop of Moscow was named the first Patriarch of Moscow and All Russia and thus became the primate of the Russian Orthodox Church. The role was abolished by Peter the Great in 1723 but reinstated by the Church after the revolution of October 1917.

Tonsuring: The act of trimming the hair in preparation for entry into monastic life, also performed on kings at the moment of death as a sign of their renunciation of worldly power.

Tsarevich: The son of a tsar.

Tsarevna: The daughter of a tsar.

Tsaritsa: The wife or widow of a tsar.

Varangian: The Varangians were Viking warrior-traders who plied the rivers and waterways of Russia as early as the ninth century. One of them, Rurik, founded the city of Novgorod in 862 and gave his name to the first ruling dynasty in Russia.

Voevoda: Literally "warlord," the title of a high military commander.

A SCENE FROM *Faust*

FAUST

I'm bored, demon.

MEPHISTOPHELES
What of it, Faust?
Such is the line that's drawn for you,
And nobody can step across it.
All reasonable creatures are bored:
Some are too lazy, some too busy;
One has faith, another's lost it;
This one had no time for pleasure,
That one had too much of it,
And all of them yawn their lives away,
And the yawning grave awaits you all.
So you yawn, too.

FAUST
A stale joke!
Better find me some way or other
To get distracted.

MEPHISTOPHELES
Content yourself
With the proofs of reason. Write this down
In your notebook: *Fastidium est quies*,
"Boredom is the soul's repose."

I'm a psychologist . . . that is science! . . .
Tell me, when have you not been bored?
Think, search. When you dozed off
Over Virgil, and a good birching
Brought you to your senses again?
Or when you crowned those lighthearted,
Easygoing girls with roses
And amid the riotous noise devoted
The ardor of a drunken night to them?
Or was it when you immersed yourself
In the most high-minded dreams,
In the obscure abyss of knowledge?
But, I remember, it was just then,
Out of boredom, like a harlequin,
From the flames you finally summoned . . . me.
I minced around like a petty demon,
Trying hard to cheer you up,
Took you to witches and to spirits;
And what then? It was all for naught.
You wanted fame—and so you got it;
You wanted love—and fell in love.
You took every tribute life could offer,
But were you happy?

FAUST
Enough of that,
Don't aggravate my secret wound.
In the depths of knowledge there's no life—
I cursed the lying light of knowledge,
And glory . . . its arbitrary ray
Is elusive. Worldly honor is

As meaningless as dreams . . . But yet
There is an outright blessing: the union
Of two souls . . .

MEPHISTOPHELES
And the first tryst,
Am I right? But allow me to inquire:
Whom are you pleased to have in mind—
Might it be Gretchen?

FAUST
O wondrous dream!
O the purest flame of love!
There, there—in the shade of rustling trees,
Where the streams were burbling sweetly—
There, resting my weary head
Upon her lovely breast, there
I was happy . . .

MEPHISTOPHELES
Lord of heaven!
You're raving, Faust, and in broad daylight!
Your servile memory deceives you.
Wasn't it I who took the trouble
To provide you with that wondrous beauty?
And in the darkest hour of night
To bring her together with you? That time
I enjoyed the fruit of my endeavor
All by myself, how the two of you . . .
I remember everything. While your beauty
Was in rapture, was in ecstasy,
You in your restlessness of soul

Already sank into reflections
(And you and I have demonstrated
That reflection is the germ of boredom).
And do you know, my philosopher,
What you were thinking at that time
When no one thinks? Shall I tell you?

FAUST

Speak. What was it?

MEPHISTOPHELES
You were thinking:
My submissive lamb! How greedily
I desired you! How cleverly I stirred up
The dreams in a simple maiden's heart!
She innocently gave herself
To generous, devoted love . . .
Why then is my breast now filled
With anguish and with hateful boredom? . . .
Having drunk my fill of pleasure,
I gaze at the victim of my whim
With irrepressible revulsion:
Just so does a careless fool,
Venturing upon a wicked deed,
Murder a beggar in the forest
And then curse the shabby corpse;
Just so does a debaucher glance
Sidelong at his boughten beauty,
After his hasty satisfaction . . .
Thus after all that went before
You arrived at one conclusion . . .

FAUST

Away with you, infernal creature!
Out of my sight!

MEPHISTOPHELES

With pleasure, sir.
Just set me up some little task:
You see, I don't dare part from you
If I have nothing else at hand.
I really hate to waste my time.

FAUST

Say, what's that whiteness over there?

MEPHISTOPHELES

It's a three-masted Spanish schooner,
Preparing to dock itself in Holland:
It's carrying some three hundred scoundrels,
Two apes, several chests of gold,
A bountiful load of chocolate, and
A fashionable illness: a recent gift
To you.

FAUST

Go drown it all.

MEPHISTOPHELES

At once.

(He disappears.)

Little Tragedies

THE MISERLY KNIGHT

(Scenes from Shenstone's tragicomedy The Covetous Knight*)*

SCENE I

In a Tower
Albert and Ivan

ALBERT

However much the tournament may cost,
I will appear. Show me the helmet, Ivan.

Ivan hands him the helmet.

There's a hole in it. It's ruined. Impossible
To wear it. I will have to buy a new one.
What a stroke! Damn that Count Delorge!

IVAN

And you rewarded him quite handsomely:
After the way you knocked him from his stirrups,

He lay unconscious a whole day and night—
It's unlikely he's recovered.

ALBERT
                    But he lost nothing;
His Venetian breastplate is intact,
And as for his breast, it won't cost him a cent;
He won't have to buy himself a new one.
Why didn't I take his helmet off right there!
And I would have, if the ladies and the duke
Had not made me ashamed. That damned count!
He'd have done better to put a hole in my head.
I also need some clothes. Last time the knights
Were all sitting there in satin and in velvet;
I was the only one wearing armor
At the duke's table. I excused myself, saying
I had landed in the tournament by chance.
What will I say now? Oh, poverty,
Poverty! How it humiliates the heart!
When Delorge's heavy lance pierced through
My helmet and he went galloping by me,
And I, my head uncovered, put the spurs
To my Emir, raced, fell upon the count,
And threw him twenty paces down the road
Like a little page boy; when all the ladies
Rose from their seats, when Clotilda herself,
Covering her face, cried out involuntarily,
And the heralds loudly praised my stroke—
No one gave any thought to the real reason
For my valor and for my astounding strength!
I was furious about my damaged helmet.

What caused my heroism?—Miserliness.
Yes! It's not hard to be infected by it,
Living under the same roof as my father.
How is my poor Emir?

IVAN

He's still limping.
You won't be able to ride him yet.

ALBERT

Ah, well,
No help for it: in that case I'll buy Chestnut.
They're not asking very much for him.

IVAN

Not very much, only we have no money.

ALBERT

What does that worthless Solomon have to say?

IVAN

He says he cannot go on lending you
Money on credit without a pledge.

ALBERT

A pledge!
Where the devil am I to get a pledge?

IVAN

I told him that.

ALBERT

And he?

IVAN

He groans and cringes.

ALBERT

You should have told him that my father is
As rich as a Jew himself, and sooner or later
I will inherit everything.

IVAN

I told him that.

ALBERT

And so?

IVAN

He cringes and groans.

ALBERT

What a pain!

IVAN

He wanted to come himself.

ALBERT

Well, God be praised!
I won't let him go away without a ransom.

Knocking at the door.

Who's there?

The Jew enters.

JEW

Your humble servant.

ALBERT

Ah, my friend!
The cursed Jew, the worthy Solomon,

Kindly come in: so I've heard that you
Have no trust in your debtor.

JEW

Oh, gracious knight,
I swear to you, I would . . . but I really can't.
Where will I get the money? I've gone bankrupt
From all my zealous helping of you knights.
None of you pays me back. I've come to ask
If you might not repay some part of . . .

ALBERT

Robber!
If I ever found myself with any money,
Would I be mucking around with you? Enough,
Don't be stubborn, my dear Solomon;
Give me gold. Dish me out a hundred,
Or else I'll have your pockets searched.

JEW

A hundred!
Where would I get a hundred in cash!

ALBERT

Listen:
Aren't you ashamed not to give your friends
A little help?

JEW

I swear . . .

ALBERT

Enough, enough,
So you demand a pledge? What balderdash!

What sort of pledge do you want from me? A pigskin?
If I had any pledge, I would have sold it
Long ago. Or is the word of a knight
Not enough for a dog like you?

JEW

                              Your word,
While you're alive, means very, very much.
Like a talisman, it will unlock for you
All the coffers of the wealthy Flemish.
But if you hand it over to a poor Jew
Like me, and meanwhile, God forbid, you die,
In my hands it will turn out like the key
To a strongbox that's been thrown into the sea.

ALBERT

Can it be that my father will outlive me?

JEW

Who knows? The numbering of our days is not for us.
Yesterday's blossoming youth is dead today,
And here four bent old men are bearing him
On their stooping shoulders to the grave.
The baron's in good health. God willing, he
May live another ten or twenty years,
Maybe even twenty-five or thirty.

ALBERT

You're lying, Jew: thirty years from now
I will turn fifty, what use will I have
For money then?

JEW

For money? Money

Is always of use to us at any age.

But a young man seeks a nimble servant in it

And sends it here and there unsparingly.

An old man sees it as a trusty friend

And cherishes it like the apple of his eye.

ALBERT

Oh, my father sees no friend or servant in it,

But a master, and it is he who serves it.

And how does he serve it? Like an Algerian slave,

Like a chained-up dog. In an unheated kennel

He lives, drinks water, eats dry crusts,

Doesn't sleep all night, runs back and forth and barks.

And meanwhile the gold just lies there peacefully

In its coffers. Quiet! If ever it should come

To be my servant, it won't lie there for long.

JEW

Yes, at the baron's funeral

More money will be shed than tears. God grant

You get to inherit soon.

ALBERT

Amen to that!

JEW

Or maybe . . .

ALBERT

What?

JEW

It just occurred to me
That there's a means . . .

ALBERT

What sort of means?

JEW

It's this—
Among my acquaintances there's a little old man,
A Jew, a poor apothecary . . .

ALBERT

A moneylender
Like yourself, or more honorable than that?

JEW

No, knight, Tobias has a different trade.
He concocts these drops . . . it's truly amazing
How they work.

ALBERT

What are they to me?

JEW

Add them to a glass of water . . . just three drops,
They have no taste, no noticeable color;
With no stomach cramps, no nausea, no pain,
The man dies.

ALBERT

The old man deals in poison.

JEW

Yes, also in poison.

ALBERT

So instead of money,
You're offering me two hundred vials of poison,
One gold piece per vial. Is that it?

JEW

Mock me all you like—no, what I meant . . .
Maybe you . . . I thought it might be time
For the baron to die.

ALBERT

What! Poison my father!
And me, his son, you dared . . . Seize him, Ivan!
And me you dared! . . . Do you know, you Hebrew soul,
You dog, you serpent, I'll hang you from the gatepost
Right now.

JEW

I'm sorry! Forgive me, I was joking.

ALBERT

Ivan, the rope.

JEW

I . . . I was joking. I've brought the money.

ALBERT

Get out, you dog!

The Jew exits.

That's what I'm driven to
By my father's miserliness! The Jew dares make me
Such an offer! Give me a glass of wine,
I'm trembling all over . . . Even so, Ivan,

I need the money. Run after the cursed Jew,
Take his gold. And fetch me an ink bottle.
I'll write the crook a receipt.
But don't bring the Judas here . . . Or, no, wait.
His gold will stink of poison, like the silver
Of his predecessor . . . I asked you for wine.

IVAN

We don't have a drop of wine.

ALBERT

                    What about the case
That Raymond sent me as a gift from Spain?

IVAN

Yesterday I brought the last bottle of it
To the ailing blacksmith.

ALBERT

                    Yes, I remember, I know . . .
Then give me water. What a cursed life!
No, I've decided—I'll go and seek defense
From the duke himself: let him force my father
To keep me like a son, not like a mouse
Born under the floorboards.

SCENE II
A Cellar

THE BARON

Just as a young rake waits for a rendezvous
With some deceitful and promiscuous wench,
Or a foolish one he has seduced, so I
Have waited all day long to come down here
To my secret cellar, to my faithful coffers.
Oh, happy day! for on this day I can
Pour a handful of gold that I have saved
Into the sixth coffer (it's not yet full).
It doesn't seem like much, but bit by bit
My treasure grows. I read somewhere
About a king who once ordered his troops
To bring handfuls of dirt to make a heap,
And so a proud hill rose—and from its top
The king could happily survey
The valley below, studded with white tents,
And the sea, where ships went flitting by.
So I, bringing my regular contributions
In poor handfuls to the cellar here,

Have raised up my hill—and from its height
I can gaze on all that's in my power.
What isn't in my power? Like some demon,
I can rule over all the world from here;
At my mere wish, a palace will arise;
In my splendid gardens a throng of nymphs
Will frisk about; the muses will offer me
Their tribute, a proud genius be my slave,
And virtue and sleepless labor
Will humbly wait for my reward. I'll whistle
And bloody villainy will come crawling to me,
Obedient, timid, and will lick my hand,
And look into my eyes, seeking in them
Signs of my will. Everything obeys me,
I obey nothing; I'm above all desires;
I'm calm; I know my power, and that knowledge
Suffices me . . .

He looks at his gold.

                    Not very much, it seems,
But how many human cares, deceits, entreaties,
Tears and curses its heaviness embodies!
There's an old doubloon here . . . this one. Today
A widow gave it to me, but before that
She spent half the day with her three children
Kneeling and wailing outside my window. It rained,
Then stopped, then rained again. The shamming woman
Wouldn't budge. I could have chased her away,
But some voice whispered to me
That she had come to pay her husband's debt,

So as not to find herself in jail tomorrow.
And this one? This was brought to me by Thibaut—
A good-for-nothing, a cheat. Where did he get it?
He stole it, of course; or else, maybe there
On the high road, at night, in the woods . . .
Yes! if all the tears, the blood and sweat
Shed for all that is kept hidden here
Rose up suddenly from the depths of the earth,
There would be a flood, and I would drown
Here in my trusty cellar. But now to business.

He is about to open the coffer.

Each time I'm about to open my coffer,
I break into a sweat and start to tremble.
It's not from fear (No! Who am I afraid of?
I have my sword: honorable Damascus
Will answer for gold), but my heart is wrung
By some inexplicable feeling . . .
Doctors have assured us there are people
Who take pleasure in murder. When I put
The key into the keyhole, I feel the same
As they must feel when they thrust a knife
Into their victim: pleasure and fear together.

He opens the coffer.

Here is my bliss!

He pours the money in.

                    In you go. Enough
Of wandering the world, serving men's passions and needs.
Sleep here the sleep of power and of peace,
The way the gods sleep in the deepest heavens . . .
I want to have myself a feast today:
I will light a candle before each coffer,
And open them all, and stand here among them
Gazing down upon the glittering heaps.

He lights the candles and opens the coffers one after another.

I reign! . . . Ah, see, what magical glitter!
My domain is strong, obedient to me;
In it is happiness, in it my honor and glory!
I reign . . . but who will come after me
To take power over it? My inheritor!
A madcap, a youthful squanderer,
A boon companion of dissolute libertines!
The moment I die, he—he!—will come down here
Under these peaceful, silent vaults,
With a throng of greedy, fawning friends.
Having stolen the keys from my dead body,
He will laughingly open all the coffers,
And laying hands upon my treasure, pour it
Into satin pockets full of holes.
He'll smash the sacred vessels,
He'll mix the royal holy balm with mud—
He'll squander . . . And what right does he have?
As if I gained it all for nothing,
Or jokingly, like a gambler who shakes dice
And rakes in heaps of money? Who can tell

How much it cost me of bitter self-restraint,
Of curbed passions, of oppressive thoughts,
Of daily cares and nights of sleeplessness?
Or will my son tell me that my heart
Is overgrown with moss, that I knew
No desires, felt no pangs of conscience—
Conscience, a sharp-clawed beast
That tears your heart, an uninvited guest,
A wearisome companion, a crude creditor,
A witch who makes the moon go dark and graves
Open in confusion and send forth their dead? . . .
No, first suffer for your riches, then we'll see
Whether the wretch starts wasting what he's gained
By his own sweat and blood.
Oh, if only I could shield my cellar
From unworthy gazes! Oh, if only
I could come from my grave, a watchful shadow,
Sit on a coffer, and protect my treasure
From the living, as I am doing now! . . .

SCENE III

In the Palace
Albert, Duke

ALBERT

Believe me, my lord, I've suffered a long time
From the shame of bitter poverty. Were it not
Extreme, you would not be hearing my complaint.

DUKE

I believe you, I believe you: a noble knight,
Such as you are, would not accuse his father
Were it not extreme. Few are so depraved . . .
Be at peace: I have sent for your father
To talk to him face-to-face, without ado.
I'm waiting for him. We haven't seen each other
For a long time now. He was my grandfather's friend.
I remember, when I was still a child,
He used to sit me on his horse and cover me
With his heavy helmet, as if with a bell.

Looks out the window.

Who is that?
Is it not him?

ALBERT

Yes, it is him, my lord.

DUKE

Go to that room. I'll send for you.

Exit Albert; enter Baron.

Well, Baron,
I'm glad to see you looking so hale and hearty.

BARON

I'm happy, my lord, that I was well enough
To present myself in answer to your summons.

DUKE

It's long, Baron, long since we've seen each other.
Do you remember me?

BARON

I, my lord?
I see you as if it were today. Oh, you
Were a frisky child. The late duke used to say to me:
Philippe (he always called me Philippe),
What do you think? Eh? In twenty years,
By god, you and I will both look stupid
Next to this little fellow . . . Next to you,
That is . . .

DUKE

Well, now we can renew
Our acquaintance. You have forgotten my court.

BARON

I'm old now, my lord: what is there for me
To do at court? You are young; you like
Tournaments, feasts. I am no longer fit
For such things. If God sends war, then I
Am ready, groaning, to mount my horse again;
And I still have strength enough to draw
My old sword for you with a trembling hand.

DUKE

Baron, your fervor is well known to us;
You were a friend to my grandfather; my father
Respected you. And I have always considered you
A brave and faithful knight—but let's sit down.
Do you have children, Baron?

BARON

          I have a son.

DUKE

Why do I not see him here with me?
You're weary of the court, but for him it's fitting,
Given his age and rank, to be with us.

BARON

My son dislikes noisy social life;
He has a shy and gloomy character—
Forever wandering the woods around the castle
Like a young deer.

DUKE

          It isn't good for him
To be so shy. We'll quickly get him used

To gaiety, to balls and tournaments.
Send him to me; set up an allowance
For your son that is suitable to his rank . . .
You're frowning—perhaps you're tired from the road?

BARON

I'm not tired, my lord; but you embarrass me.
I did not want to confess it to you, but
You force me to tell something about my son
That I would rather have kept hidden from you.
Unfortunately, my lord, he is not worthy
Either of your favors or of your attention.
He throws away his youth in raucousness,
In lowly vices . . .

DUKE

That, Baron, is because
He is alone. A solitary life
And idleness are the ruin of young people.
Send him to us: he will soon forget
The habits he acquired miles from nowhere.

BARON

Forgive me, but really, good my lord,
I cannot possibly consent to that . . .

DUKE

Why not?

BARON

Spare an old man . . .

DUKE

I insist: reveal to me
The reason for your refusal.

BARON

I'm very angry
With my son.

DUKE

For what?

BARON

For a wicked crime.

DUKE

And what, tell me, does this crime consist of?

BARON

Spare me, Duke . . .

DUKE

This is very strange,
Or are you ashamed of him?

BARON

Yes . . . I'm ashamed . . .

DUKE

But what has he done?

BARON

He . . . he wanted
To kill me.

DUKE

To kill you! Why, then I will have him
Hauled into court, as the blackest villain.

BARON

I cannot prove it, though I know
That he most certainly desires my death,
Though I know that he made an attempt
On me . . .

DUKE

To do what?

BARON

To rob me.

Albert rushes into the room.

ALBERT

You're lying, Baron!

DUKE

(to the son)

How dare you? . . .

BARON

You, here! You, you dared! . . .
You could say such words to me, your father! . . .
I'm lying! And that before the duke, our master! . . .
To me, me . . . am I not a knight?

ALBERT

You're a liar.

BARON

Righteous God, Your thunder has not yet struck!
Then pick this up and let the sword decide!

He throws down his gauntlet; his son quickly picks it up.

ALBERT

Thank you. This is the first gift from my father.

DUKE

What's this I see? What has been done before me?
A son has accepted the challenge of his old father!
And it is in such days that I must wear
The ducal chain! Silence: you, old madman,
And you, you tiger cub! Enough!

To the son.

                 Drop that;
Give me that gauntlet.

He takes it.

ALBERT
(aside)
Too bad.

DUKE

He just sank his claws into it!—the monster!
Get out: do not dare appear before my eyes
Until I summon you myself.

Exit Albert.

Wretched old man,
Aren't you ashamed . . .

BARON
Forgive me, my lord,
I'm unable to stand up . . . my knees are weak . . .
I'm suffocating! . . . suffocating! . . . Where are my keys?
My keys, my keys! . . .

DUKE
He's dead. Oh, God!
What a terrible age, what terrible hearts!

MOZART AND SALIERI

SCENE I

A Room

SALIERI

They all say there's no justice here on earth.
But neither is there justice up above.
For me that is as clear as a simple scale.
I was born with a love of art; while still a child,
When I heard the organ resound
Aloft in our old church, I was entranced—
Tears, involuntary and sweet, poured down.
From early on, I abandoned idle amusements;
Studies, apart from music, bored me;
I stubbornly and scornfully rejected them,
And turned to music only. The first step
Is hard, and the first path tedious. I overcame
The early adversities. I made of craft
The foundation stone of art. I became a craftsman.
My fingers I endowed with dutiful, dry dexterity
And my ear with precision. Once the sounds
Were dead, I opened music like a corpse,

Verified harmony with algebra. Only then
Did I make bold, already filled with knowledge,
To allow myself the delight of creative dreams.
I started to create; but in quiet, in secret,
Not daring yet to give a thought to fame.
Often, sitting in my silent cell
Two days or three, forgetting sleep and food,
Tasting ecstasy and tears of inspiration,
I burned my work and coldly watched
How my thoughts and the sounds I'd given birth to
Went up in flames and vanished in light smoke.
What am I saying? When the great Gluck appeared
And revealed new mysteries to us
(Profound and fascinating mysteries),
Did I not drop all I had known before,
All I had loved and believed so ardently,
And follow boldly after him, without
A murmur, like someone who is lost and whom
A passerby sends off another way?
So by great effort, by persistent striving,
I finally reached high levels
In this illimitable art. Fame smiled on me;
My creations found a response in people's hearts.
I was happy: I peacefully enjoyed
My work, success, fame; just as I did
The works and the successes of my friends,
My close companions in this wondrous art.
Never did I know envy—oh, never!—
Not when Piccinni managed to captivate
The ears of primitive Parisians, nor the first time
I heard the opening sounds of *Iphigénie*.

Who in the world can say that proud Salieri
Has ever been despicably envious,
Like a snake, crushed underfoot but still alive,
Gnawing impotently at sand and dust?
No one! . . . But now—I say it myself—now
I am envious. I envy, envy deeply,
Tormentingly. —O heaven! Where is justice,
When a sacred gift, when immortal genius
Is not sent as a reward of ardent love,
Of self-denial, labor, zeal, and prayer,
But shines upon the head of a madcap,
An idle reveler? . . . Oh, Mozart, Mozart!

Enter Mozart.

MOZART

Aha! So you saw me! And here I was hoping
To play an unexpected prank on you.

SALIERI

You're here!—For how long?

MOZART

Just now. I was coming to you,
Bringing something I wanted to show you.
But passing by a tavern, suddenly
I heard a fiddle . . . No, my friend Salieri!
In all your born days you have never heard
Anything funnier . . . A blind fiddler in a tavern
Playing "Voi che sapete."* Marvelous!

* An aria from Mozart's opera *The Marriage of Figaro.*

I couldn't help it, I've brought the fiddler here
To treat you to his artfulness. —Come in!

Enter a blind old man with a fiddle.

Play us something by Mozart!

The old man plays an aria from Don Giovanni. *Mozart laughs heartily.*

                    SALIERI

And you can laugh?

                    MOZART

Ah, Salieri! Can it be that you're not laughing?

                    SALIERI

No, I'm not. When a crude dauber
Botches Raphael's Madonna, I don't laugh,
Nor when a worthless mountebank
Dishonors Alighieri with a parody.
Get out, old man.

                    MOZART
                (to the old man)
            Wait: this is for you,
Drink to my health.

The old man exits.

                    You're out of sorts today,
Salieri. I'll come back to see you
Some other time.

SALIERI

What have you brought for me?

MOZART

Nothing really; a trifle. Late last night
I was suffering from insomnia,
And two or three thoughts came to my head.
Today I jotted them down. I wanted
To hear your opinion of them; but right now
You can't be bothered with me.

SALIERI

Ah, Mozart, Mozart!
When can I not be bothered with you? Sit down;
I'm listening.

MOZART
(at the pianoforte)

Picture to yourself . . . who, then?
Well, me, for instance—only a little younger;
In love—not passionately, but slightly—
I'm with a pretty girl, or with a friend—you, for instance,
I'm happy . . . All at once a sepulchral vision,
A sudden darkness or something else like that . . .
Well, listen now.

He plays.

SALIERI

You were bringing that to me,
And meanwhile you could stop off at a tavern
And listen to a blind fiddler! —My god!
Mozart, you're not worthy of yourself.

MOZART

So it's good?

SALIERI

         What depth! What boldness, and
What just proportion! Mozart, you're a god,
And you don't know it. I know it.

MOZART

                  Hah! really?
Maybe so . . . But right now my godhood is hungry.

SALIERI

Listen: let's go and have a bite together
At the Inn of the Golden Lion.

MOZART

                Yes, why not;
Gladly. But let me go home and tell my wife
Not to hold dinner for me.

Exits.

SALIERI

            I'll be waiting.
No! I can no longer set myself against
My destiny: I'm the one who has been chosen
To stop him—otherwise all of us will perish,
All of us, the priests, the faithful servants of music,
Not just me with my obscure renown . . .
What's the use, if Mozart goes on living
And reaches new heights? Will he raise art that way?
No, it will fall again once he is gone.

He won't leave any heirs. What use is he?
Like a cherub, he brought us paradisal songs
Only to arouse a wingless yearning in us,
Children of dust, and fly away again!
Fly away, then! And the sooner the better.
Here's poison, the final gift of my Izora.
I've carried it around with me for eighteen years—
And often in that time life seemed to me
An unbearable wound, and I often sat
At the table with an unsuspecting enemy,
And never bowed to the whisper of temptation,
Though I am not a coward,
Though I am deeply sensitive to offense,
Though I have little love of life—I waited.
When the wish for death tormented me,
Why die? I thought: maybe life will offer me
Unexpected gifts; maybe I'll be visited
By ecstasy, a creative night, and inspiration;
Maybe a new Haydn will produce
Something great—and I'll delight in it . . .
Feasting with a hated guest, I'd think,
Maybe I'll find a still worse enemy;
Maybe a worse offense will strike me from
A lofty height—then you, Izora's gift,
Will not be wasted. And see, I was right!
And I have finally found my enemy,
And a new Haydn has made me drunk
With wondrous ecstasy!
Now is the time! Cherished gift of love,
Today you pass into the cup of friendship.

SCENE II

A private room in a tavern; a pianoforte.
Mozart and Salieri at the table.

SALIERI

Are you in a gloomy mood today?

MOZART

Me? No!

SALIERI

Surely, Mozart, something has upset you?
The dinner's good, the wine is excellent,
But you frown and keep silent.

MOZART

I'll confess,
My Requiem is troubling me.

SALIERI

Ah!
So you're composing a Requiem? Since when?

MOZART

Since three weeks ago. But a strange thing . . .
Didn't I tell you?

SALIERI

No.

MOZART

Listen, then.
Three weeks ago I came home late. They told me
Someone had been to see me. I don't know why,
But I spent the whole night thinking: Who could it be?
And what does he want of me? The next day
The same man came, and again he didn't find me.
On the third day I was playing on the floor
With my little boy. They called me; I went out.
A man dressed all in black bowed courteously,
Commissioned a Requiem from me, and disappeared.
I sat down at once and started writing—
And since then my black man has not come back,
And I'm glad of it: I would be sorry to part
With my work, though the Requiem is quite ready.
But meanwhile I . . .

SALIERI

What?

MOZART

I'm ashamed to confess it . . .

SALIERI

Confess what?

MOZART

My black man gives me no peace day and night.
He pursues me like a shadow everywhere.
Even now it seems to me he's sitting with us
As a third.

SALIERI

Enough! What is this childish fear?
Laugh off such empty thoughts. Beaumarchais
Used to tell me: "Listen, brother Salieri,
When dark thoughts come to you, uncork
A bottle of champagne, or else reread
The Marriage of Figaro."

MOZART

Yes! Beaumarchais,
He was your friend; you composed *Tarare* for him,
A fine thing. There is a motif in it . . .
I keep humming it to myself when I feel happy . . .
La la la la . . . Ah, is it true, Salieri,
That Beaumarchais once poisoned somebody?

SALIERI

I don't think so: he was too comical
For such occupations.

MOZART

He was a genius,
Like you and me. Genius and villainy
Are incompatible. Isn't that true?

SALIERI

You think so?

He drops the poison into Mozart's glass.

Well, drink up.

MOZART
To your health, my friend,
To the real bond between Mozart and Salieri,
Two sons of harmony.

He drinks.

SALIERI
No, wait,
Wait, wait! . . . You drank! . . . without me?

MOZART
Throws his napkin on the table.

Enough, I'm full.

Goes to the pianoforte.

Listen, Salieri, this is my Requiem.

He plays.

You're weeping?

SALIERI
These tears are flowing
For the first time: I feel both pained and pleased,
As if I've carried out a heavy duty,
As if a healing knife has just cut off
A suffering part of me. Mozart, my friend,

These tears . . . Pay no attention to them. Go on,
Quickly fill my soul with still more sounds . . .

MOZART

If only everyone could feel the power
Of harmony so well. But no: the world
Could not exist then; no one would look after
The needs of lower life; then everyone
Would give themselves entirely to free art.
There are few of us, chosen ones, lucky idlers,
Who disregard and scorn utility,
High priests of beauty alone. Isn't that so?
But I feel a bit unwell today, as if
Something's weighing on me. I'll go and sleep.
Goodbye then!

SALIERI

Goodbye.

Alone.

You will have
A long sleep, Mozart! But can he be right,
And I am not a genius? Genius and villainy
Are incompatible. No, that isn't true:
What about Buonarroti? Or is it a tale
Told by the stupid, senseless mob—and he
Who built the Vatican was not a murderer?

THE STONE GUEST

> Leporello: O statua gentilissima
> Del gran Commendatore . . .
> . . . Ah, Padrone!
> *—Don Giovanni*

SCENE I
Don Juan and Leporello

DON JUAN
We'll wait here until nightfall. Ah, at last
We have reached the gates of Madrid. And soon now
I will be flying down familiar streets,
My mustache covered with a cloak, my brows
With a hat. What do you think? Can I be known?

LEPORELLO
Oh, no! Don Juan is hard to recognize!
There's a horde of men just like him!

DON JUAN

                              Are you joking?
Who will recognize me?

LEPORELLO
                    The first watchman,
A gypsy girl, or a drunken musician,
Or your own kind, an insolent cavalier,
With a sword under his arm and a cloak on his back.

DON JUAN
There's no harm if they recognize me. Only
Let me not meet the king himself. In fact,
I'm not afraid of anyone in Madrid.

LEPORELLO
But by tomorrow it will reach the king
That without permission Don Juan has returned
From banishment to Madrid—and what, pray tell,
Will he do with you then?

DON JUAN
                    Send me back.
No, surely, they won't go cutting off my head.
I'm not a state criminal. He exiled me
Out of love; so that the murdered man's family
Would leave me in peace . . .

LEPORELLO
                    Well, that's just it!
You should have gone on peacefully sitting there.

DON JUAN

Thank you very much! I nearly died
Of boredom there. Such people, such a place!
And the sky? . . . all smoke,
And the women? You see, my foolish Leporello,
I wouldn't trade the last Andalusian farm girl
For their foremost beauty—true, at first I liked them,
With their blue eyes, their fair skin, and their modesty—
And most of all, their novelty. But, thank God,
I caught on soon enough.
I saw that it was no good dealing with them.
There's no life in them, they're all just wax dolls;
Whereas ours! . . . But listen, this place
Is familiar to us; do you recognize it?

LEPORELLO

How could I not: St. Anthony's Monastery,
I remember it very well. You used to come here,
And I would tend the horses in this grove.
A cursed duty, I must say. No,
You spent your time here much more pleasurably
Than I did, believe me.

DON JUAN
(pensively)
Poor Iñez!
She's no longer with us! And I loved her so!

LEPORELLO

Iñez!—dark-eyed . . . oh, yes, I remember.
You spent three months dangling after her,
And barely succeeded, with the devil's help.

DON JUAN

It was July . . . at night. How strangely attractive
I found her mournful gaze and the deathly pallor
Of her lips. Yes, it is strange. You, it seems,
Did not find her beautiful. And, in fact,
There was very little real beauty in her.
The eyes, the eyes alone. Yes, her gaze . . .
Never again have I met such a gaze.
And her voice was soft and weak—
As if she were ill. Her husband, I learned later,
Was a ruthless scoundrel . . . Poor Iñez! . . .

LEPORELLO

Well, so, others came after her.

DON JUAN

                    True enough.

LEPORELLO

And if we go on living, there'll be still others.

DON JUAN

That's so.

LEPORELLO

        In Madrid now, which of them
Will we be looking up?

DON JUAN

                    Oh, Laura!
I'll go running straight to her.

LEPORELLO

Well, so that's settled.

DON JUAN

Straight to her door, and if somebody's there
Already, I'll invite him to jump out the window.

LEPORELLO

Of course. Well, so we've cheered up nicely now.
Dead women don't trouble us for long.
Who's that coming here?

A monk enters.

MONK

She will arrive
Any moment now. Who's there. Doña Anna's people?

LEPORELLO

No, we're our own masters, just out taking
A little stroll.

DON JUAN

And who are you expecting?

MONK

Doña Anna will come here in a moment
To visit her husband's tomb.

DON JUAN

What! Doña Anna
De Silva! The wife of the commander
Who was killed . . . I forget by who?

MONK

By that depraved,

That shameless, godless Don Juan.

LEPORELLO

Oho!

Look at that! So the fame of Don Juan
Has made its way to a peaceful monastery,
Even the recluses sing in praise of him.

MONK

Maybe you know him?

LEPORELLO

Us? Oh, not at all.

And where is he now?

MONK

He isn't here,

He's in exile far away.

LEPORELLO

Thank God for that.

The farther the better. These philanderers
Should all be stuffed into a sack and drowned.

DON JUAN

What? What's this blather?

LEPORELLO

Quiet: I'm deliberately . . .

DON JUAN

So the commander has been buried here?

MONK

Yes, here. His wife set up a monument to him
And she comes every day to weep and pray
For the repose of his soul.

DON JUAN

What a strange widow!
And is she good-looking?

MONK

We recluses
Should not be tempted by the beauty of women,
But to lie is sinful: not even a saint
Could help acknowledging her wondrous beauty.

DON JUAN

So the dead man had reasons to be jealous.
He kept his Doña Anna locked away,
None of us has ever set eyes on her. I wonder
If she and I could have a little talk.

MONK

Oh, Doña Anna never talks with men.

DON JUAN

And with you, Father?

MONK

With me it's another matter;
I'm a monk. Ah, here she is.

Enter Doña Anna.

DOÑA ANNA
            Unlock it, Father.

MONK
At once, señora; I've been waiting for you.

Doña Anna exits with the monk.

LEPORELLO
Well, how do you find her?

DON JUAN
            I couldn't see her
Under her widow's black cowl.
I only caught a glimpse of a slender heel.

LEPORELLO
That's enough for you. Imagination
Will fill out the rest for you in a minute, faster
Than any painter. It's all the same to you
Where you begin, eyebrows or feet.

DON JUAN
                        Listen, Leporello,
I'll introduce myself to her.

LEPORELLO
            Of course!
Just what we need! You brought down the husband
And now you want to gaze at the widow's tears.
Shameless!

DON JUAN
            Anyway it's already getting dark.
Before the moon rises over us

And turns the darkness into a bright twilight,
Let's go to Madrid.

He exits.

LEPORELLO

         A Spanish grandee waits
For nightfall like a thief and fears the moon—
Oh, God, curse this life! Must I bother with him
Much longer? Really, it's beyond my strength.

SCENE II
A room. Supper at Laura's.

FIRST GUEST

I swear to you, Laura, never before
Have you performed with such perfection.
How rightly you have understood your role.

SECOND GUEST

You developed it so well! And with such power!

THIRD GUEST

With such artfulness!

LAURA

            Yes, tonight my every word
And gesture came off well. I gave myself
Freely to inspiration. The words poured out
As if they were born, not from slavish memory,
But from the heart . . .

FIRST GUEST

            True . . . And even now
Your eyes are flashing and your cheeks are flushed.

In you, Laura, the ecstasy has not passed.
Don't let it cool off fruitlessly. Sing, Laura,
Sing something.

LAURA

Give me the guitar.

She sings.

ALL

Bravo, bravo! Wonderful! Incomparable!

FIRST GUEST

Thank you, sorceress. You charm our hearts.
Of all life's pleasures, music takes second place
Only to love; but love is also melody . . .
Just look: even Carlos, your sullen guest, is moved.

SECOND GUEST

Such sounds! There is so much soul in them!
Who wrote those fine words, Laura?

LAURA

Don Juan.

DON CARLOS

What? Don Juan!

LAURA

He composed them once—
My faithful friend, my very flighty lover.

DON CARLOS

Your Don Juan is godless and a scoundrel,
And you . . . are a fool.

LAURA

Have you lost your mind?
I'll have my servants cut your throat right now,
Even if you are a Spanish grandee.

DON CARLOS

(stands up)

Send for them.

FIRST GUEST

Stop it, Laura; Don Carlos, don't be angry.
She forgot . . .

LAURA

Forgot what? That Don Juan
Killed his brother honorably in a duel?
Too bad it wasn't him.

DON CARLOS

I was stupid to get angry.

LAURA

Aha! So you yourself admit you're stupid.
Then let's make peace.

DON CARLOS

It was my fault, Laura,
Forgive me. But you know: I cannot hear
That name with equanimity . . .

LAURA

And is it my fault
That every moment that name trips from my tongue?

A GUEST

So as a sign that you're no longer angry,
Laura, sing again.

LAURA

Yes, it is time
For farewells, night has already fallen. But
What shall I sing? Ah, listen.

She sings.

ALL

Lovely! Incomparable!

LAURA

Farewell then, gentlemen.

GUESTS

Farewell, Laura.

They exit. Laura holds Don Carlos back.

LAURA

You, furious one! Stay here with me,
I've taken a liking to you. You reminded me
Of Don Juan, the way you cursed at me
And ground your teeth.

DON CARLOS

The lucky man!

So you loved him.

Laura nods her head affirmatively.

Very much?

LAURA
             Very much.

DON CARLOS
And you love him even now?

LAURA
                      At this moment?
No, I don't love him. I cannot love two men.
I now love you.

DON CARLOS
             Tell me, Laura,
How old are you?

LAURA
             Eighteen.

DON CARLOS
                You're young . . .
And will be young for five or six more years.
For some six years they will all crowd around,
Woo you, pamper you, and give you gifts,
And entertain you with evening serenades,
And on account of you, they'll kill each other
By night at the crossroads. But when your time has passed,
When your eyes sink in and your wrinkled eyelids darken,
And gray hair streaks your braid,
And you come to be known as an old woman—
What will you say then?

LAURA
                Then? But why
Think of that? What's there to talk about?
Or do you always have such thoughts? Come—

Open the balcony. How still the sky is;
The warm air is motionless, the night
Is fragrant with lemon and laurel, the bright moon
Shines in the deep, dark blueness,
And the watchman cries out drawlingly: "All's well!" . . .
Yet far away, to the north—in Paris—
It may be that the sky is covered with clouds,
A cold rain is falling and the wind blows.
But what is that to us? Listen, Carlos,
I demand at least a little smile from you . . .
—There, that's better!

DON CARLOS
My dear demon!

Knocking.

DON JUAN
Hey! Laura!

LAURA
Who's there? Whose voice is that?

DON JUAN
Open up . . .

LAURA
It can't be! . . . My God! . . .

She opens the door; Don Juan enters.

DON JUAN
Greetings . . .

LAURA

Don Juan! . . .

Laura throws herself on his neck.

DON CARLOS

What! Don Juan! . . .

DON JUAN

Laura, my dear friend! . . .

Kisses her.

Who's here with you, my Laura?

DON CARLOS

It is I,

Don Carlos.

DON JUAN

What an unexpected meeting!
Tomorrow I'll be entirely at your service.

DON CARLOS

No! Now—this minute.

LAURA

Stop, Don Carlos!
You're not in the street, you are in my house.
Kindly get out.

DON CARLOS

(not listening to her)

I'm waiting. Well, what then,
You do have a sword.

DON JUAN

If you are so impatient,

As you please.

They fight.

LAURA

Ay! Ay! Juan! . . .

She throws herself on the bed. Don Carlos falls.

DON JUAN

Get up, Laura, it's over.

LAURA

What is it?
Killed? Wonderful! And in my own room!
What am I to do now, you rake, you devil?
Where am I to throw him?

DON JUAN

Maybe he's still

Alive.

LAURA
(examining the body)

Oh, yes, alive! Look, curse you,
You stabbed him right in the heart—no fear you'd miss,
And no blood flows from the triangular wound,
And he's no longer breathing—how about that?

DON JUAN

What could I do? He asked for it.

LAURA

Eh, Don Juan,

It's annoying, really. Eternal mischief
And never to blame . . . Where have you come from now?
Have you been here long?

DON JUAN

No, I just arrived,

And on the quiet—I have not been pardoned.

LAURA

And you remembered at once about your Laura?
All well and good. But enough of that,
I don't believe it. You happened to walk by
And saw my house.

DON JUAN

Not so, my Laura,

Ask Leporello. I'm staying outside town,
In a cursed flophouse. I came to Madrid
Looking for my Laura.

He kisses her.

LAURA

My dear friend! . . .

Wait . . . this dead man! . . . What can we do with him?

DON JUAN

Leave him here: toward dawn, early,
I'll take him away wrapped up in a cloak
And lay him out at the crossroads.

LAURA

Only

Make sure nobody catches sight of you.
It's a good thing you didn't show yourself
A minute earlier. Your friends were here
Having supper with me. They just left.
What if you had found them here?

DON JUAN

How long

Have you loved him, Laura?

LAURA

Who? You must be raving.

DON JUAN

Confess, how many times have you betrayed me
In my absence?

LAURA

And what of you, you scapegrace?

DON JUAN

Tell me . . . No, we'll talk about it after . . .

SCENE III

The Commander's Monument

DON JUAN

It's all for the best: by chance I killed Don Carlos,
Now, like a humble recluse, I hide here
And every day I see my lovely widow,
And she, it seems, has noticed me. So far
We have kept our distance, but today
I'll strike up a conversation with her; it's time.
What to begin with? "May I be so bold . . ."
Or no: "Señora . . ." Bah! I'll say whatever
Comes to my head, without any preparation,
I'll be the improviser of a love song . . .
But it's time she came. I think the commander
Is bored without her. Look at the colossus
They've made of him. What shoulders. A real Hercules! . . .
Yet the late man himself was small and frail,
Even on tiptoe he could not have reached
The nose of his own statue. When he and I
Came at each other behind the Escorial,
He impaled himself upon my sword

Like a dragonfly on a pin—and yet he was
Proud and brave—and stern of spirit . . . Ah!
It's her.

Enter Doña Anna.

DOÑA ANNA

He's here again. My Father,
I am distracting you from your reflections.
Forgive me.

DON JUAN

It is I who should ask forgiveness
Of you, señora. Perhaps I keep your sorrow
From freely pouring out.

DOÑA ANNA

No, my Father,
My sorrow is within me. In your presence
My prayers may rise humbly up to heaven,
And I beg you to join your voice with them.

DON JUAN

What, me, me pray with you, Doña Anna!
No, I am not worthy of such a lot.
I would not dare repeat your holy prayer
With my sinful lips—I'll only look at you
In awe, from a distance, when bending down
Quietly, you scatter your dark hair
Over the pale marble—and I fancy
An angel has secretly visited this tomb.
In my confused heart I can find no prayers.
I only marvel silently and think—

Happy is he whose cold marble is warmed
By her heavenly breath and wetted with the tears
Of her love.

DOÑA ANNA

What strange talk!

DON JUAN

Señora?

DOÑA ANNA

It seems . . . you've forgotten . . .

DON JUAN

What? That I am
An unworthy hermit? That my sinful voice
Ought not to ring out so loudly here?

DOÑA ANNA

It seems to me . . . I didn't understand . . .

DON JUAN

Ah, I see: you know, you know it all!

DOÑA ANNA

What do I know?

DON JUAN

That I am not a monk—
I beg your forgiveness at your feet.

DOÑA ANNA

Oh, God! Get up, get up . . . Who are you then?

DON JUAN

A wretch, the victim of a hopeless passion.

DOÑA ANNA

Oh my God! and here beside this tomb!
Go away!

DON JUAN

One minute, Doña Anna,
Just one minute!

DOÑA ANNA

What if someone comes! . . .

DON JUAN

The grille is locked. Give me just one minute!

DOÑA ANNA

Well? So? What are you asking for?

DON JUAN

Death.
Oh, let me die right now here at your feet,
And let my poor remains be buried,
Not near the remains that are so dear to you,
No, not close—but somewhere farther off,
There—by the gates—just at the threshold,
So that my tombstone might be brushed
By your light foot or garment, when you come
To loose your locks and weep over this proud grave.

DOÑA ANNA

You've lost your mind.

DON JUAN

Is it a sign of madness,
Doña Anna, to wish for death? Were I

A madman, I would wish to go on living,
I would hope that I might touch your heart
With tender love; were I a madman,
I'd spend my nights under your balcony,
Disturbing your sleep with my serenades.
I would not be in hiding; on the contrary,
I'd try to attract your attention everywhere.
Were I a madman, I would not be suffering
In silence . . .

DOÑA ANNA
So you call this silence?

DON JUAN
Chance, Doña Anna, chance carried me away.
Or else you'd never have learned of my sad secret.

DOÑA ANNA
And have you loved me long?

DON JUAN
                              Long or not,
I don't know myself. But only since then
Have I known the value of this momentary life
And learned the meaning of the word *happiness*.

DOÑA ANNA
Go away—you are a dangerous man.

DON JUAN
Dangerous? How?

DOÑA ANNA
I'm afraid to listen to you.

DON JUAN

I'll be quiet; only do not drive away
The one who so delights in seeing you.
I nourish no bold hopes, nor do I make
Any demands on you, but I must see you,
So long as I'm condemned to live.

DOÑA ANNA

Go—

This is no place for such talk, such madness.
Come to me tomorrow. If you swear
To be just as respectful of me, I'll receive you;
But later, in the evening—since I've been a widow
I have seen no one.

DON JUAN

Angel Doña Anna!

May God comfort you, as you yourself today
Have comforted a wretched sufferer.

DOÑA ANNA

Go away now.

DON JUAN

Just a minute more.

DOÑA ANNA

No, obviously I must leave . . . besides, my mind
Is not inclined to prayer. You've distracted me
With worldly talk; for a long, long time
My ear has been unaccustomed to it. Tomorrow
I will receive you.

DON JUAN

I dare not believe it,
I dare not give myself to my happiness . . .
Tomorrow I will see you! —And not here,
Not secretly!

DOÑA ANNA

Yes, tomorrow, tomorrow.
What is your name?

DON JUAN

Diego de Calvado.

DOÑA ANNA

Goodbye, Don Diego.

She exits.

DON JUAN

Leporello!

Enter Leporello.

LEPORELLO

At your service.

DON JUAN

My dear Leporello!
I'm happy! . . . "Tomorrow, later in the evening . . ."
My Leporello, tomorrow—get things ready . . .
I'm happy as a little child!

LEPORELLO

You spoke
With Doña Anna? And maybe she said

A couple of nice words to you, or else
You gave her your blessing.

DON JUAN

No, Leporello, no,
She arranged a rendezvous with me!

LEPORELLO

Really!
Oh, widows, you are all the same.

DON JUAN

I'm happy!
I'm ready to sing, I'll gladly embrace the whole world!

LEPORELLO

And the commander? What will he say about it?

DON JUAN

Do you think he will be jealous? Surely not;
He is a reasonable man, and surely he has
Calmed down since he died.

LEPORELLO

No; look at his statue.

DON JUAN

What about it?

LEPORELLO

It seems to be watching you,
And it's angry.

DON JUAN

Go to it, Leporello,
Ask it to come and visit me—no, not me,
But Doña Anna tomorrow.

LEPORELLO

Invite a statue
To be your guest! What for?

DON JUAN

Well, surely
Not in order to talk things over with him—
Ask the statue to come to Doña Anna's
Tomorrow, late at night, and to stand guard
By the door.

LEPORELLO

You're in the mood for making jokes,
And with whom!

DON JUAN

Go on now.

LEPORELLO

But . . .

DON JUAN

Go on.

LEPORELLO

Most glorious, most beautiful of statues!
My master Don Juan humbly asks of you
The honor of . . . God, no, I just can't do it,
I'm afraid.

DON JUAN

Coward! I'll give you one! . . .

LEPORELLO

Wait, allow me.

My master Don Juan asks that you come tomorrow,
Late at night, to call upon your spouse
And stand by the door . . .

The statue nods in assent.

Aiee!

DON JUAN

What is it?

LEPORELLO

Aiee, aiee! . . .

Aiee, aiee . . . I'm dying! . . .

DON JUAN

What's the matter with you?

LEPORELLO
(*nodding his head*)

The statue . . . *aiee! . . .*

DON JUAN

You're nodding!

LEPORELLO

No, not me,

It's him!

DON JUAN

What are you driveling about?

LEPORELLO

Look for yourself.

DON JUAN

Step aside, you good-for-nothing.

(to the statue)

I invite you, Commander, to come to your widow's house,
Where I will be tomorrow, and stand guard
At her door. Well, so? Will you be there?

The statue nods again.

Oh, God!

LEPORELLO

What did I tell you? . . .

DON JUAN

Let's get out of here.

SCENE IV

Doña Anna's Room
Don Juan and Doña Anna

DOÑA ANNA

I have received you, Don Diego; only
I am afraid that my sad conversation
Will bore you: I'm a poor widow, I still remember
My loss. Tears mingle with my smiles,
As on an April day. Why are you silent?

DON JUAN

I'm silently and deeply savoring
The thought of being here alone
With lovely Doña Anna. Here, not there—
Not by the grave of that fortunate dead man—
And I see you now no longer on your knees
Before your marble husband.

DOÑA ANNA

               So you're jealous,
Don Diego. Even in his grave
My husband torments you?

DON JUAN

I should not be jealous.
It was you who chose him.

DOÑA ANNA

No, my mother
Told me to give my hand to Don Alvaro.
We were poor, Don Alvaro was rich.

DON JUAN

Lucky man! He brought empty treasures
To lay at the goddess's feet, and that was how
He tasted the bliss of paradise. If only
I had known you earlier, with what rapture
I would have given my rank, my wealth, my all,
All for a single favorable glance;
I'd be the slave of your most sacred will,
I'd make a study of all your little whims,
So as to anticipate them; so that your life
Would be one continuous enchantment.
Alas! Destiny decided otherwise.

DOÑA ANNA

Stop it, Diego: I am sinning now
By listening to you—I cannot love you,
A widow must be faithful to the very grave.
If only you could know how Don Alvaro
Loved me! Oh, Don Alvaro surely
Would never have received an amorous lady,
Were he a widower. He would be faithful
To his wedded love.

DON JUAN

Do not torment my heart,
Doña Anna, eternally remembering
Your husband. You have punished me enough,
Though I may deserve such punishment.

DOÑA ANNA

For what?
You're not bound by a sacred bond to anyone.
—Isn't that so? In loving me,
You're in the right before both me and heaven.

DON JUAN

Before you! My God!

DOÑA ANNA

Can you be guilty
Before me? Tell me, of what.

DON JUAN

No! No, never.

DOÑA ANNA

What is this, Diego? Are you in the wrong before me?
How so, tell me.

DON JUAN

No! Not for anything!

DOÑA ANNA

This is strange, Diego: I ask you, I demand.

DON JUAN

No, no.

DOÑA ANNA

Ah! So this is your obedience
To my will! And what was it you said to me
Just now? That you wished to be my slave.
I'm getting angry, Diego: answer me,
What are you guilty of before me?

DON JUAN

                  I don't dare,
You'll hate me for it.

DOÑA ANNA

          No, no. I forgive you
Beforehand, but I want to know . . .

DON JUAN

               You will not
Want to know such a terrible, murderous secret.

DOÑA ANNA

Terrible! You're tormenting me.
I'm trembling with curiosity—what is it?
And how can you offend me? I didn't know you—
I have no enemies and I never had.
My husband's killer is the only one.

DON JUAN
(to himself)

Now things are coming to a head!
Tell me, this unfortunate Don Juan—
Do you know him?

DOÑA ANNA

        No, I have never seen him.

DON JUAN

Do you nurse a hatred of him in your heart?

DOÑA ANNA

By a debt of honor. But you're distracting me
From my question, Don Diego—I demand . . .

DON JUAN

What if you were to meet Don Juan?

DOÑA ANNA

                  I would plunge
A dagger in the villain's heart.

DON JUAN

             Where is your dagger,
Doña Anna? Here is my breast.

DOÑA ANNA

           Diego!
What are you doing?

DON JUAN

        I'm not Diego, I'm Juan.

DOÑA ANNA

Oh, God! No, it can't be, I don't believe it.

DON JUAN

I am Don Juan.

DOÑA ANNA

        Not true.

DON JUAN

            I killed your husband;
And I don't regret it—I feel no remorse.

DOÑA ANNA

What am I hearing? No, no, it cannot be.

DON JUAN

I am Don Juan, and I love you.

DOÑA ANNA
(*swooning*)

Where am I? . . . Where am I? I'm fainting, fainting.

DON JUAN

Good God!

What is it? What's the matter, Doña Anna?
Stand up, stand up, wake up, come to your senses:
Your Diego, your slave, is at your feet.

DOÑA ANNA

Let go of me!
(*weakly*)

Oh, you are my enemy—you have taken from me
Everything in life that I . . .

DON JUAN

Dearest creature!

I'm ready to redeem my stroke with anything,
Here at your feet I only await your command:
Order me—and I'll die; order me—and I'll breathe
For you alone . . .

DOÑA ANNA

So this is Don Juan . . .

DON JUAN

It's true, is it not, that he was described to you
As a villain, a monster. Oh, Doña Anna,
Maybe the rumor's not entirely false,
Maybe many evil burdens have worn out
My conscience. So for a long time I was
An obedient disciple of depravity,
But ever since I first set eyes on you,
It seems that I've been totally reborn.
In loving you, I fell in love with virtue,
And for the first time I humbly bent
My trembling knees before it.

DOÑA ANNA

           Oh, Don Juan
Is a sweet talker—I know, I've heard as much;
He is a sly seducer. You, they say,
Are a godless corrupter, a veritable demon.
How many poor women have you ruined?

DON JUAN

I never loved a single one of them.

DOÑA ANNA

And I'm to believe Don Juan has fallen in love
For the first time, that he is not seeking
A new victim in me?

DON JUAN

           If I wanted to deceive you,
Would I have confessed and told you that name
You cannot bear to hear? Where do you see
Any premeditation and treachery in that?

DOÑA ANNA

Who knows you? But how could you come here;
Here you could be recognized, and your death
Would be inevitable.

DON JUAN
What is death?

For the sweet moment of seeing you,
I would give my life without a murmur.

DOÑA ANNA

But how will you ever leave here, imprudent man!

DON JUAN
(kissing her hands)

So you're concerned about poor Juan's life!
And there's no hatred in your heavenly soul,
Doña Anna?

DOÑA ANNA
Ah, if only I could hate you!

But in any case, we must part.

DON JUAN
And when

Shall we see each other again?

DOÑA ANNA
I don't know.

Someday.

DON JUAN
Maybe tomorrow?

DOÑA ANNA
Where?

DON JUAN
Here.

DOÑA ANNA
Oh, Don Juan, I feel so weak of heart.

DON JUAN
In pledge of your forgiveness, a peaceful kiss . . .

DOÑA ANNA
It's time, go now.

DON JUAN
Just one cold, peaceful . . .

DOÑA ANNA
You're so insistent! There, take it.
What's that knocking? . . . Oh, hide yourself, Don Juan.

DON JUAN
Goodbye, until tomorrow, my dearest friend.

He exits and runs back in.

Ah! . . .

DOÑA ANNA
What's wrong? Ah! . . .

Enter the statue of the Commander. Doña Anna faints.

STATUE
I've come at your invitation.

DON JUAN

Oh, God! Doña Anna!

STATUE

Let her be.
It is all over. You're trembling, Don Juan.

DON JUAN

Me? No. I invited you and am glad to see you.

STATUE

Give me your hand.

DON JUAN

Here . . . Oh, how heavy
His stone handshake is! Let go of me,
Let go—let go of my hand . . .
I'm lost—it's all over—oh, Doña Anna!

They fall through the floor.

A FEAST IN A TIME OF PLAGUE
(After The City of the Plague, *a tragedy by John Wilson, 1816)*
The street. A set table. Several men and women feasting.

A YOUNG MAN

Most honored chairman, I speak in memory
Of a certain man well known to all of us,
Of one whose jokes, amusing anecdotes,
Witty repartees and observations,
Sarcastic in their playful earnestness,
Enlivened our table talk and drove away
The darkness that our guest, the pestilence,
Brings down upon the most brilliant of minds.
Only two days ago our general laughter
Hailed his stories; it is impossible
That we in our merry feasting
Could have forgotten Jackson! Here his chair
Stands empty, as if it were awaiting
The merrymaker—but he's already gone
Down to his cold dwelling underground . . .
No more eloquent tongue has ever yet
Fallen silent in sepulchral dust;

But many of us are still living, and we have
No reason to be sorrowful. Therefore
I propose that we drink to his memory
With a merry clinking of glasses, with loud cheers,
As if he were alive.

CHAIRMAN
He was the first
To leave our circle. Let us drink in silence
To his honor.

YOUNG MAN
So be it!

They all drink silently.

CHAIRMAN
Your voice, my dear, brings out the sounds
Of your own native songs with wild perfection.
Sing for us, Mary, slowly and mournfully,
So we can then go back to merrymaking
More madly still, like one who was estranged
From earthly being by some sort of vision.

MARY
(sings)
Once upon a time our township
Flourished in the world:
Every Sunday in those days
The church of God was filled;
The children in the noisy schoolhouse
Raised their voices high,
And across the bright field flashed
The sickle and quick scythe.

Now the church is emptied out,
The school is locked up tight;
The dark grove is deserted, the idle
Field is overripe;
And the village stands alone here
Like a house burnt down.
All's quiet—only the graveyard is
Not silent, not forlorn.

Every moment the dead are brought
And the living wail,
Begging God in fearfulness
To grant rest to their souls!
Every moment space is needed,
And to one another,
The graves, like a frightened flock of sheep,
Huddle close together!

If my springtime's truly destined
For an early grave,
You, whom I loved so deeply, you
Who entranced me with your love,
I pray you: to your Jenny's body
Do not dare go near,
Nor touch her dead lips with your kiss,
But follow her from afar.

And then up and leave the village!
Go away somewhere,
Find a place where you can sweeten
And ease your soul's despair.

And when the plague is past and gone,
Come visit my poor dust,
For even in heaven Edmund will
Remain in Jenny's breast.

CHAIRMAN

Our thanks to you, dear melancholy Mary,
Our thanks to you for your most plaintive song!
In days gone by, it seems, a plague like this
Came calling on your hills and hollows, raising
Pitiful wails on the banks of streams and brooks
That now flow on quite peacefully and gaily
Through the wild paradise of your native land;
And that dark year in which so many victims
Fell, courageous, kind, and beautiful,
Leaving but the faintest memory of themselves
In some sort of simple shepherd's song,
Sorrowful and pleasing . . . No, there's nothing
That saddens us more amidst our merrymaking
Than a languid sound that echoes in the heart!

MARY

Oh, if only I had never sung
Outside the cottage where my parents raised me!
How they loved to listen to their Mary;
It seems to me that I can hear myself
Singing by the threshold of my birthplace.
My voice was sweeter in those days: it was
The voice of innocence . . .

LOUISA
Such songs
Are not in fashion now! Yet there are still
Such simple souls: only too glad to melt
At women's tears and to believe them blindly.
She is quite certain that her tearful gaze
Is irresistible—and if she thought
The same of her laughter, she would be sure
To start smiling. Walsingham has praised
Loud northern beauties: so here she is
Moaning away. Oh, how I despise
The yellow color of this Scottish hair!

CHAIRMAN
Listen: I hear the clatter of wagon wheels!

A cart passes filled with dead bodies. The driver is a black man.

Aha! Louisa's fainted; to hear her talk,
I would have thought she had a man's heart in her.
But look—the tough are weaker than the tender,
And fear lives in the soul worn out by passions!
Mary, splash water on her face. She's better.

MARY
Sister of my sorrow and disgrace,
Lean on my breast.

LOUISA
(coming to her senses)
A terrible demon
Came to me in a dream: all black, white-eyed . . .

He beckoned me to get into his cart.
Dead people lay in it, jabbering away
In some terrible unknown language . . .
Tell me: Was it really all a dream?
Did a cart drive by?

YOUNG MAN

Oh, come, Louisa,
Cheer up now—though this whole street of ours
Is a silent refuge from death, a haven
For feasts, not disturbed by anything.
You know this black cart has the right to drive
Everywhere. So we must let it pass!
Listen, Walsingham: to stop the arguments
And the consequences of such female swoons,
Sing us a song, a free and lively song,
Not inspired by Scottish melancholy,
But a riotous and bacchic song,
Born over a cup of foaming wine.

CHAIRMAN

I don't know any, but I'll sing a hymn
In honor of the plague—last night I wrote it.
After we parted a strange fit of rhymes
Came over me for the first time in my life!
Hear how it's suited to my husky voice.

MANY VOICES

A hymn in honor of the plague! Listen to him!
A hymn in honor of the plague! Splendid! Bravo, bravo!

CHAIRMAN
(sings)

When like a bold chieftain
Mighty Winter swoops
Upon us with his troops
Of shaggy frost and snow—
We meet him with crackling fires
And merry feasting's glow.

The terrible queen, the Plague,
Now goes against us all,
And hopes for a rich haul;
And her gravedigger's spade
Keeps rapping at our window . . .
Will none come to our aid?

As on mischievous Winter,
On the Plague we'll shut the door,
Light lamps and drink still more,
Merrily our minds to drown
And in a whirl of feasts and dancing,
Exalt the Plague's renown.

There's inebriation in battle,
On the brink of a black abyss,
In huge waves and churning darkness
Of the furious ocean's rage,
In the Arabian desert's sandstorm,
And in the breathing of the Plague.

All, all that threatens death,
For the hearts of mortals hides
Inexplicable delights—
Even a pledge of eternal life!
Happy one who can find and know them
Amid such storm and strife.

And so—praise to thee, Plague,
We fear not the grave's dark pall,
We're undaunted by your call!
Our foaming cups we raise
And drink the rose-maiden's breath—
Though it, too, be filled with Plague!

Enter an old priest.

PRIEST

Godless feast, godless madmen!
With your feasting and licentious songs
You mindlessly befoul the mournful silence
That death is everywhere disseminating!
Amid the horror of tearful funerals,
Amid pale faces I pray at the graveyard,
But these hateful ecstasies of yours
Disturb the silence of the sepulchers
And shake dirt onto the bodies of the dead!
Had not the prayers of old men and wives
Sanctified the common pit of death,
I might now think that demons were tormenting
The damned spirit of some godless man
And laughing as they dragged him down to darkness.

SEVERAL VOICES

He speaks of hell with such great expertise!
Back with you, old man! Back to where you came from!

PRIEST

I here adjure you by the sacred blood
Of the Savior who was crucified for us:
Break off this monstrous feasting, if you wish
To meet again in heaven the dear souls
Of those you've lost. Go back to your homes!

CHAIRMAN

Our homes are sad for us—what youth likes best
Is joy.

PRIEST

Is that you, Walsingham? The same
Who, on your knees, in tears, three weeks ago,
Embraced your mother's corpse, and with loud howling
Beat upon her grave? Or do you think
She's not now weeping, weeping bitterly
Up there in heaven, looking down upon
Her feasting son, in a debauched feast,
Hearing your voice singing wild songs
In the midst of holy prayers and heavy sighs?
Follow me now!

CHAIRMAN

Why have you come
To trouble me? I may not, no, I must not
Go with you: I'm held here by despair,
By a terrible memory, by the awareness
Of my own lawlessness, and by the horror

Of the dead emptiness that meets me in my house—
And by the novelty of this mad merriment,
And the blessed poison of this cup,
And the caresses (Lord forgive me)
Of this lost but lovely creature . . . My mother's shade
Won't draw me out of here—it is too late—
I hear your voice calling me—I recognize
Your attempts to save me . . . go in peace, old man,
But cursed be the one who follows you!

MANY VOICES

Bravo, bravo! Worthy chairman!
There's a sermon for you! Go now! Go!

PRIEST

Matilda's pure spirit is calling you!

CHAIRMAN
(stands up)

Swear to me, raising your pale and withered hand
Toward heaven, that you will let that name
Remain forever silent in the grave!
Oh, if only I could hide this spectacle
From her immortal eyes! There was a time
When she thought me pure and proud and free—
And she knew paradise in my embrace . . .
Where am I? Holy child of light! I see you
There where my fallen spirit can
No longer reach . . .

A WOMAN'S VOICE
He's lost his mind—
He's raving about his long-buried wife!

PRIEST

Come, come . . .

CHAIRMAN
My Father, for God's sake,
Let me be!

PRIEST
May the Lord save you!
Farewell and forgive, my son.

*He exits. The feasting goes on. The chairman remains sunk
in deep thought.*

The Water Nymph

THE BANKS OF THE DNIEPER. A MILL.

The miller and his daughter

MILLER

Oh, all of you young girls, you're all so stupid!
If you have the luck to meet some worthy man,
Not a commoner, you should bind him to you
Tightly. How? With sensible, honorable behavior;
Entice him with sternness, then with tenderness,
Chancing now and then, as if offhand,
To speak of a wedding—and above all else
Look after your maiden's honor—a priceless treasure;
Like a word—once gone, it cannot be called back.
And if there's no hope for a wedding, then
At least you can gain something for yourself,
Or some profit for your family; your thought should be:
"He won't go on loving and pampering me forever."
But no! you don't even dream of doing right!
You lose your wits at once; you're glad enough
To sate his whims for nothing; you're quite ready
To hang on your sweetheart's neck all day—and he,
Your sweetheart, up and vanishes without a trace;

And you're left with nothing. Oh, you're all so stupid!
Haven't I told you a hundred times: Eh, daughter,
Watch out; don't be a fool, don't miss your chance,
Don't let the prince slip, don't ruin yourself for nothing.
—And what came of it? . . . So sit there now
And weep forever over what can't be brought back.

DAUGHTER

But why do you think he abandoned me?

MILLER

                                        What do you mean,
Why? And just how many times a week
Would he come to the mill? Eh? Every blessed day
And sometimes even twice a day—but then
He began to come more rarely, rarely, and now
It's nine days since we've seen him. What do you say?

DAUGHTER

He's busy; does he have so little to do?
He's not a miller, water doesn't work for him.
He often says of all jobs his is the hardest.

MILLER

Go on, believe him. When princes take up work,
What kind of work is it? Hunting hares and foxes,
And feasting, and antagonizing their neighbors,
And sweet-talking you poor foolish girls.
So he's the one who works—oh, poor fellow!
While water works for me! . . . and I get no rest,
Day or night, and then look: here there's rot,
There there's a leak, it all needs to be mended.
If you could talk the prince out of some money,
At least a little, for repairs, that would be better.

DAUGHTER

Ah!

MILLER

What is it?

DAUGHTER

Listen! I hear the hoofbeats
Of his horse . . . It's him, it's him!

MILLER

Be careful, daughter,
Don't forget my good advice, remember . . .

DAUGHTER

He's here, he's here!

The prince enters. His squire leads the horse away.

PRINCE

Greetings, my dear friend.
Greetings, miller.

MILLER

Most gracious prince,
Welcome to you. It's a long, long time
Since we have seen your bright eyes. I will go
And prepare some refreshments for you.

Exits.

DAUGHTER

Ahh,
At last you've remembered me! Aren't you ashamed
To torment me so cruelly, making me wait so long

For no reason? What thoughts went through my head!
What fearful visions of you frightened me!
I thought your horse had carried you into a swamp
Or over a cliff, that a bear had come upon you
In the thick of a forest, or that you were sick,
Or that you had stopped loving me—but thank God!
You're alive and well, and love me as before;
Isn't that so?

PRINCE

As before, my angel,
No, still more than before.

HIS BELOVED

And yet you're sad.
What's wrong?

PRINCE

Me, sad? No, you're imagining it.
It's always a joy for me to see you.

SHE

No.
When you feel joy you come rushing to me
And cry out: "Where's my dove? What is she doing?"
Then you kiss me and ask: "Are you glad to see me,
And were you expecting me so early?" But today
You listen to me silently, you don't embrace me,
Don't kiss my eyes. Something must be troubling you.
What is it? Can it be you're angry with me?

PRINCE

I don't want to pretend that it is nothing.
You're right: in my heart I bear a heavy sorrow,

And your loving caresses cannot dispel it,
Or lighten it, or even share it with me.

SHE

It pains me not to be saddened by your sadness—
Tell me your secret. If you permit, I'll weep;
If not, I won't annoy you with a single tear.

PRINCE

Why put it off? The sooner the better.
My dear friend, you know that in this world
There's no lasting happiness: neither noble birth,
Nor beauty, nor strength, nor riches—nothing can save us
From misfortune. And we—isn't it so, my dove?—
We were happy; or at least I was happy
With you, with your love. And whatever happens
In the future, wherever I am, I'll always remember
You, my friend; nothing in the world
Can replace what I'm losing.

SHE

I still don't understand
Your words, but I'm frightened. Destiny threatens us,
It is preparing some unknown calamity,
Perhaps a parting.

PRINCE

You have guessed right.
We are destined to part.

SHE

But who can part us?
Can't I follow you everywhere? I'll put on boys' clothes,
I'll serve you faithfully no matter where you go,
On the march, or in war—I'm not afraid of war—

So long as I can see you. No, no, I don't believe it.
Either you're trying to find out my thoughts,
Or else you're playing a silly joke on me.

PRINCE

No, joking isn't on my mind today,
And I have no need to find out your thoughts.
I'm not preparing for a distant journey,
Or for war—I am staying home,
But I must part from you forever.

SHE

Wait,
Now I understand it all . . . You're getting married.

The prince says nothing.

You're getting married! . . .

PRINCE

What can I do?
Judge for yourself. Princes are not free,
Like young girls—it isn't by the heart
That they choose a mate, but by the calculation
Of others, for the profit of other people.
God and time will console you in your grief.
Do not forget me; take this headband
As a memento—let me put it on you.
I've also brought a necklace—here, take it.
And one more thing: I promised it to your father.
Give it to him.

He hands her a sack of gold.

Farewell.

SHE
Wait, I must tell you . . .
I don't remember what.

PRINCE
Try to remember.

SHE
For you, I'm ready for everything . . . no, that's not it . . .
Wait—it can't be that you could really abandon me
Forever . . . No, not that, either . . . Ah, yes! . . . I remember:
Today I felt your child stir under my heart.

PRINCE
Poor girl! What can we do? At least for his sake,
Take care of yourself; I will not abandon
Either you or your child. Perhaps after a while
I'll come to visit you myself. Be comforted,
Don't grieve. Let me embrace you one last time.

As he exits:

Ohh! it's over—now my heart feels lighter.
I was expecting a storm, but things worked out
Quite calmly.

He exits. She stands immobile. The miller enters.

MILLER
If you please, sir,
Come into the mill . . . but where is he?

Tell me, where is our prince? Ah, ah, ah!
What a headband! All studded with precious stones!
See how they shine! And a necklace, too! . . . Well, well,
I'd call that a princely gift. Oh, he's a benefactor!
And what's this now? A poke! Is there money in it?
Why are you standing there, not answering,
Not letting out one little word? Or maybe
You're dumbstruck by some sudden joy, or else
You've turned into a post?

DAUGHTER

                    I don't believe it,
It can't be. I loved him so. Is he a beast?
Is his heart overgrown with fur?

MILLER

                    Who do you mean?

DAUGHTER

Tell me, dear father, how could I have angered him?
Or maybe in one short week my beauty vanished?
Or else he drank some poison?

MILLER

                    What's the matter?

DAUGHTER

Dear father, he's gone. That's him galloping off!
And, madwoman that I am, I let him go,
I didn't seize his coat, I didn't cling
To his horse's bridle! Let him chop off my arms
In his anger, let him trample me under his horse
Right now!

MILLER

You're raving!

DAUGHTER

You see, princes aren't free,
Like young girls, they do not choose a wife
After their heart . . . but clearly they are free
To lure, to promise, to gently weep and say:
"I'll bring you to my bright palace, to a secret chamber,
And deck you out in brocade and crimson velvet."
They're free to instruct a poor girl to get up
At midnight at a whistle and sit till dawn
Behind the mill. The princely heart delights
In our distress, and then goodbye, my dove,
Go wherever you like, love whom you fancy.

MILLER

Ah, so that's it.

DAUGHTER

Who is his bride?
Who has he traded me for? Oh, I'll find out,
I'll get my hands on her. I'll tell the wicked girl:
Drop the prince—you see, two she-wolves can't
Go rubbing shoulders in the same ravine.

MILLER

Fool!
If the prince has taken a bride, who can prevent him?
There you have it. Didn't I tell you . . .

DAUGHTER

And he
Could give me gifts, like a decent man—such gifts!

And money! He thought he could buy his way out,
He wanted to silverplate my tongue
So that no bad rumors would circulate about him
And get as far as his young wife. Ah, I forgot,
He told me to give you this money, in return
For being so good to him, for allowing your daughter
To drag after him, instead of being strict . . .
My ruin has turned out profitable for you.

She hands him the sack.

FATHER
(in tears)

So I've come to that! What has God let me hear!
It's wrong to reproach your own father so bitterly.
You are the only child I have in the world,
You are the only delight of my old age.
How could I not pamper you?
God has punished me for being weak
In fulfilling my parental duty.

DAUGHTER
                    Oh, I'm choking!
A cold snake is strangling me . . . He has ensnared me
With a snake, a snake, and not a string of pearls . . .

She tears off the necklace.

MILLER

Come to your senses!

DAUGHTER
This is how
I'll tear you off, wicked snake, who took him from me!

MILLER
You're raving, really raving.

DAUGHTER
(takes off the headband)
Here is my crown,
The crown of my disgrace! Here is what
The evil fiend crowned me with, when I renounced
All that was dear to me. We're no longer married.
Away with you, my crown!

She throws the headband into the Dnieper.

It is all over now.

She throws herself into the river.

OLD MAN
(falls down)
Oh, woe, woe is me!

THE PRINCE'S PALACE
The Wedding. The prince and his bride sit at the table.
Guests. A girls chorus.

MATCHMAKER

We round off the wedding with a merry feast.
So, long live the prince and his young princess.
God grant you live in love and harmony,
And that we banquet with you very often.
Why are you so quiet, pretty girls?
Why are you so silent, my white swans?
Have you no songs left? Have your throats gone dry from
  singing?

CHORUS

Matchmaker, matchmaker,
Dear witless matchmaker!
He went to make a match,
Wound up in a melon patch,
Spilled a whole barrel of ale,
Watered a row of kale.
Before a fence he bowed.

To a post he prayed out loud:
Post, dear post, you know,
Show us the way to go,
We have to find the bride.
Dear matchmaker, just think,
Open your purse—clink, clink—
The coins are all ajingle,
And we pretty girls all atingle.

MATCHMAKER

What teasers you are, to pick out such a song!
Here, here, take it, don't blame the matchmaker.

He gives the girls money.

A VOICE

Over stones, over yellow sand the swift river races,
And in the swift river swim two little fish,
Two little fish, two small common roaches.
And have you overheard, my sister fish,
Our news, the river news of yesterday?
How one of our young girls just drowned herself,
And cursed her sweetheart as she drifted down?

MATCHMAKER

My beauties! what kind of song is that?
It doesn't seem meant for weddings—no.
Who chose that song? Eh?

GIRLS

Not me—not me —
Not us . . .

MATCHMAKER

Who sang it, then?

Whispering and commotion among the girls.

PRINCE

I know who.

He gets up from the table and quietly speaks to his squire.

She slipped herself in here. Quickly take her away.
And then find out who dared to let her in.

The squire goes to the girls.

(*sits down, to himself*)

She may be ready to raise such an uproar
That I won't know where to hide myself from shame.

SQUIRE

I didn't find her.

PRINCE

Keep looking. She's here, I know.
It was she who sang that song.

GUEST

Ah, what mead!

It hits you in the head and in the feet.
Too bad it's bitter: it could use some sweetening.

The newlyweds kiss. A weak cry is heard.

PRINCE

That's her! A cry of jealousy.

(*to the squire*)

Well, so?

SQUIRE

I didn't find her anywhere.

PRINCE

Fool.

BEST MAN
(rising)

Isn't it time we handed the princess to her husband
And showered the newlyweds with hops in the doorway?

They all rise.

BRIDESMAID

Of course it's time. Bring in the roasted capon.

*The newlyweds eat the capon, then are showered with hops and
led to the bedroom.*

Princess, dear heart, don't weep, don't be afraid,
Obey your husband.

*The newlyweds go to the bedroom. The guests all leave, except for
the best man and the bridesmaid.*

BEST MAN

Where's the wine jug?

I'll be riding back and forth under their window
All night, so I need some wine to fortify me.

BRIDESMAID
(pours him a glass)

Here, have yourself a drink.

BEST MAN

Oof! Thank you.
It all came off quite well, don't you agree?
The wedding couldn't have been better.

BRIDESMAID

Yes, thank God,
It all came off quite well, save for one thing.

BEST MAN

And what was that?

BRIDESMAID

That song wasn't good.
It wasn't a wedding song, it was God knows what.

BEST MAN

These young girls—they just can't help themselves,
They've got to pull mischief. What a thing to do,
To trouble the prince's wedding like that on purpose.
Well, I must go and saddle up my horse.
Goodbye, dear girl.

He exits.

BRIDESMAID

Ah, I'm so upset!
Something wasn't right about this wedding.

THE PRINCESS'S ROOM
The princess and her nanny

PRINCESS

Listen—that sounds like a horn. No, he's not coming.
Ah, nanny, while he was still my suitor,
He wouldn't move a step away from me,
He never used to take his eyes off me.
We're married now, and everything has changed.
He rouses me early, orders his horse saddled,
And rides off God knows where until nightfall.
He comes back, murmurs a sweet word in my ear,
And pats my face lightly with his hand.

NANNY

Dear princess, a man's just like a rooster:
Cock-a-doodle-doo! Flap-flap of the wings,
And off he goes. But a woman's like a poor hen:
Just sit there by yourself and hatch your chicks.
When he courts, he can't have enough of sitting;
Doesn't eat or drink, just goes on gawking.
He gets married—and then the chores begin.

He has to pay calls on his many neighbors,
Or else to go out hunting with his falcons,
Or else some dratted war takes him away.
Here, there—he never just sits at home.

PRINCESS

What do you think, nanny? Might he not have
Some secret sweetheart?

NANNY

                    Enough, don't make things up.
Who could he possibly exchange you for?
You've got it all: incomparable beauty,
Fine breeding, and good sense. Think about it:
Where, if not in you, will he ever find
Such treasures?

PRINCESS

              If only God would hear my prayers
And send me children! Then I would be able
To attach my husband to me again . . . Ah!
The yard is full of hunters. My husband's back.
Why don't I see him?

A hunter enters.

                    The prince, where is he?

HUNTER

The prince told us all to go home.

PRINCESS

                    But where is he?

HUNTER

He stayed alone in the forest, on the bank of the Dnieper.

PRINCESS

And you dared to leave the prince there all alone,
Good servants that you are! Go back at once,
Gallop to him at once! Tell him I sent you.

The hunter exits.

Ah, my God! In the forest at night
Wild beasts, and wicked men, and wood demons roam—
Trouble's not far off. Quick, light a candle
Before the icon.

NANNY

At once, my bright one, at once . . .

THE DNIEPER
Night

WATER NYMPHS
In a merry crowd
We come up by night
From the watery depths
To the warm moonlight.
In the night we love to leave
The darkness of the riverbed,
The surface of the stream to cleave
With the thrust of our free heads,
To greet each other with loud cries,
To disturb the ringing air,
And to fluff up and let dry
Our green and water-sodden hair.

ONE NYMPH
Hush, hush! There is something hiding
Under the bushes, in the gloom.

ANOTHER

And on the bank there's someone striding
Between us and the sickle moon.

They hide.

PRINCE

Familiar, melancholy places! I recognize
The things around me—here is the mill,
A ruin now; the merry noise of the wheels
Is silent, the millstone is idle—the old man
Has evidently died. He didn't mourn
His poor daughter for long.
A path meandered here—all overgrown now,
It's a long time since anyone has come here;
There was a garden with a fence around it—
Can it have turned into this leafy grove?
Ah, here's our oak tree. Here she embraced me
And fell silent, downcast . . . Can it be? . . .

He goes to the tree; its leaves are falling.

What does this mean? The leaves fade and curl up,
And, rustling, they pour down on me like ashes.
The oak stands there before me, bare and black,
Like a cursed tree.

An old man enters, in rags, half-naked.

OLD MAN
Greetings, son-in-law.

PRINCE

Who are you?

OLD MAN

A local raven.

PRINCE

Can it be?

It's the miller.

OLD MAN

I'm no miller! I sold my mill
To petty demons and for safekeeping,
Gave the cash to my wise daughter, a water nymph.
It's buried in the sand of the river Dnieper.
A one-eyed fish is keeping watch on it.

PRINCE

The poor fellow's mad. The thoughts in his head
Are all scattered, like clouds after a storm.

OLD MAN

Why is it you didn't come to us yesterday?
We had a feast and were expecting you.

PRINCE

Who was expecting me?

OLD MAN

Who? My daughter, of course.
You know, I look at all this through my fingers
And let you have it your way: she can sit
Even all night with you, until cockcrow,
I won't say a word.

PRINCE

Poor old miller!

OLD MAN

What kind of miller am I? I told you,
I'm a raven, not a miller. It was a miracle:
When she threw herself into the river (you remember?),
I ran after her and wanted to jump off
That cliff, when suddenly I felt two strong wings
Sprout from under my arms, and they held me up.
Since then I've been flying here and there,
Now I peck at a cow's carcass, now I sit
By someone's grave, cawing.

PRINCE

What a pity!
And who looks after you?

OLD MAN

Yes, it's not a bad thing,
Having someone to look after me. I've grown old
And mischievous. Thankfully, I'm looked after
By a little water nymph.

PRINCE

Who?

OLD MAN

My granddaughter.

PRINCE

It's impossible to make sense of him. Old man,
In this forest you'll die of hunger or else be eaten

By some wild beast. Don't you want to come with me
And live in my palace?

OLD MAN
              In your palace? No, thank you!
You'll lure me there, and then you very well
May strangle me with a necklace. Here I live,
I eat, and I'm free. No, I don't want your palace.

He exits.

PRINCE
And it's all my fault! How terrible it is
To lose your mind. It's much better to die.
We look upon a dead man with respect,
We pray for him. Death makes us all his equals.
But a man deprived of reason is no longer
A man. The gift of speech is useless to him,
He has no control over words, beasts recognize him
As their brother, people make fun of him,
Anyone can offend him, God doesn't judge him.
Wretched man! The very sight of him
Has sharpened all the pain of repentance in me!

The hunter enters.

HUNTER
Here he is. It was a hard job finding him!

PRINCE
What are you doing here?

HUNTER

The princess sent us.

She feared for you.

PRINCE

Her attention is unbearable.

Am I a child? Can't I take a step without a nanny?

He exits. Water nymphs come up out of the water.

NYMPHS

So, sisters, now the field is clear,

Shall we not quickly overtake them?

Filling their noble steeds with fear,

And whistling, laughing, splashing, break them?

It's late. How dark the woods are growing,

Cold is the water in its depths,

In the village cocks are crowing,

And the waning moon has set.

ONE NYMPH

A moment longer, sisters dear.

ANOTHER

No, no more, no more, no more.

Our queen, our sister so severe,

Is waiting for us by the shore.

They disappear.

THE BOTTOM OF THE DNIEPER

The palace of the water nymphs.
The nymphs spin yarn beside their queen.

THE NYMPH QUEEN

Leave off your spinning, sisters. The sun has set.
A pillar of moonlight shines on us. Enough.
Swim up to frolic under the open sky,
And don't lay a hand on anyone today.
Don't dare to tickle any passerby.
Don't weigh down any fisherman's net with slime
And seaweed, or lure some little child
Into the water with stories about fish.

A little nymph enters.

Where have you been?

DAUGHTER

I went out on dry land
To see Grandfather. He keeps asking me
To pick up the money from the river bottom

That he threw into it once upon a time.
I've searched, but I don't know what money is.
So I brought him a handful of bright-colored shells.
He was very glad.

NYMPH

Crazy pinchfist!
Listen, daughter. I'm counting on you now.
A man will come down to our bank today.
Watch out for him, go to meet him. We're related.
He's your father.

DAUGHTER

The one who abandoned you
And married a woman?

NYMPH

The very same. Be nice, cuddle up to him,
And tell him all you've learned from me about
Your birth; tell about me, too. And if he asks
Whether I have forgotten him or not,
Say that I still remember him and love him,
And wait for him. Do you understand me?

DAUGHTER

Oh yes, I do.

NYMPH

Go, then.
(Alone)
Since that time
When I madly threw myself into the water,
A desperate and scorned young thing,

And came to myself at the bottom of the Dnieper
Turned into a cold and powerful water nymph,
Seven long years have passed—and every day
I contemplate revenge . . .
Now it seems my hour has come at last.

THE RIVERBANK

PRINCE

An invincible power draws me against my will
To this melancholy riverbank. Everything here
Reminds me of the past and of the dear,
Though sad, story of my beautiful, free youth.
Here once upon a time love used to meet me,
Free, ardent love; and I was happy.
Madman! . . . That I could renounce my happiness
So lightly! Yesterday's encounter revived in me
Such mournful, mournful thoughts. Unhappy father!
How terrible for him! Perhaps I'll meet him
Today, and he'll agree to leave the forest
And move to live with us . . .

A little water nymph steps out on the bank.

What's this I see?
Where have you come from, lovely little child?

Angelo

PART ONE

I

In one of the towns of happy Italy
There once ruled a kindly old Duke,
The loving father of his people, a friend
Of peace, a friend of truth, the arts, and learning.
But supreme power does not bear with weak hands,
And he was much too given to kindness. The people
Loved him and did not fear him in the least.
The punitive law slumbered in his courts,
Like an aged beast no longer fit for hunting.
Deep in his unmalicious heart the Duke
Felt it, and it upset him. He saw clearly
That grandchildren from day to day grew worse
Than their grandparents, that babies bit the breasts
Of nurses, that justice sat with folded arms,
And only the lazy did not flick its nose.

II

Often the kindly Duke, disturbed by conscience,
Wished to reinstate the neglected order.
But how? The obvious evil, long endured,
Seemed permitted by the silent law,
And to punish it suddenly would be most unfair
And strange—especially coming from the one
Who had encouraged it by his own indulgence.
What to do? The Duke endured, reflected,
And at last resolved that for a time
He would give the burden of supreme power
Into another's hands, so that suddenly,
Through punishment, the new ruler could establish
Firm order and be both tough and strict.

III

There was a certain Angelo, experienced,
Not new to the art of ruling, a man
Of stern habits, pale from work, study, and fasting,
Known everywhere for the strictness of his morals,
Held in on all sides by legal fencing,
With a frowning face and an inflexible will.
This man the Duke appointed as his governor,
And, arming him with terror and clothing him with mercy,
He handed his unlimited power over to him.
And the man, avoiding tiresome attention,

Not bidding farewell to anyone, incognito,
Set off alone, like a knight-errant of old.

IV

Angelo had only just entered his governance,
And everything took a different course at once.
The rusted springs began to work again.
The law rose up, clutching evil in its claws.
On Fridays in the crowded public squares,
Grown silent from fear, executions were performed,
And the common folk began to scratch their heads
And said, "Aha, this one's not like that one."

V

Among the laws forgotten in those days
There was a cruel one: this law prescribed
Death to an adulterer. No one in the town
Remembered or had heard of such a sentence.
Grim Angelo unearthed it from the massive law code,
And to put fear into the local rakes,
Brought it to light, to be enforced again,
Sternly telling his assistants: "It is time
We frightened evil. The people are spoiled, they take
Their habits for rights, and freely sneak around
The law like mice around a yawning lion.
The law should not become a ragged scarecrow
Which even birds are finally not afraid of."

VI

Thus Angelo unwittingly made everyone tremble.
The people murmured, the flighty young ones laughed,
Not sparing the strict nobleman in their jokes,
While dancing giddily on the edge of the abyss.
The first to have his head fall under the axe
Was reckless Claudio, a young patrician.
In hopes of mending all his troubles in time,
And presenting to the world not a lover, but a wife,
He managed to seduce the gentle Julietta
And bend her to the mysteries of lawless love.
But the consequences unfortunately became clear;
The young lovers were caught by witnesses,
Their mutual shame was exposed in the court,
And the young man was sentenced by the law.

VII

The wretched boy, hearing the cruel verdict,
His head hanging, went back to the prison,
Unwittingly inspiring pity in everyone,
And lamenting bitterly. Suddenly he meets up
With Lucio, a carefree philanderer,
A scapegrace, a feisty liar, but good-hearted.
"Friend," said Claudio, "I beg you! don't say no:
Go to the convent, to my sister. Tell her
That I am faced with death; let her make haste
To save me, ask her friends to intercede,

Or even go to the governor herself.
In her, Lucio, there is much art and intelligence,
God gave both sweetness and persuasion to her speech,
Though even without speeches, a weeping girl
Softens people's hearts." "Of course! I'll tell her,"
The philanderer answered, and set out at once
For the convent.

VIII

Young Isabella

Was sitting at that time with a senior nun.
She was to be tonsured the next day
And was talking about it with her spiritual elder.
Suddenly Lucio rang and came in. The novice,
Fingering her rosary, greeted him at the grille:
"Who is it you would like to see?" "Dear maiden
(And, judging by your rosy cheeks, I'm sure
You are indeed a maiden), might you tell
The beautiful Isabella
That her unfortunate brother has sent me to her?"
"Unfortunate! . . . Why? What's wrong? Tell me straight out:
I'm Claudio's sister." "No, really? Glad to meet you.
He sends his heartfelt greetings. The trouble is:
He's in prison." "What for?" "For something I myself
Would give thanks for, my beauty,
And there would be no punishment at all."
(Here he went off into detailed descriptions,
Somewhat uncouth in their nakedness
For the virginal ears of the young recluse,

But the girl heard him out attentively,
With no sweet pretense to modesty and anger.
Her soul was pure as air. She could not be
Embarrassed by a world unknown to her,
By its vanity and idle talk.) "Now," he said,
"It remains for you to move Angelo with pleading,
And that is what your brother asks of you."
"My God," the girl replied,
"If only my words could be of any use! . . .
But I doubt it; my strength will not hold out . . ."
"Doubts are our enemies," he objected hotly.
"The traitors try to frighten us with failure
And keep us from attaining our true good.
Go to Angelo, and I tell you this,
If a girl kneels before a man, and begs and weeps,
Like a god, he will give her everything she wants."

IX

The girl, asking leave of her superior,
Hastened with zealous Lucio to the governor
And, going on her knees before him,
Humbly began to plead her brother's cause.
"Young lady," the gentleman replied severely,
"You cannot save him; your brother has lived his life;
He is to die." Weeping, Isabella
Bowed before him and was about to leave,
But good Lucio held the young lady back.
"Don't give up like that," he whispered to her,

"Ask him again; throw yourself at his feet,
Seize his cloak, sob; tears, laments,
You must now make use of all the means
Of women's art. You are much too cold,
As if you're talking about some petty trifle.
Of course, in that case, there really is no point.
Don't give up now! Go on!"

X

Once more
She bashfully began her zealous pleading
Before the hard-hearted keeper of the law.
"Believe me," she said, "neither a king's crown,
Nor a governor's sword, nor a judge's mantle,
Nor a general's baton—none of these distinctions—
Nothing adorns the rulers of the earth
So much as mercy. It raises them aloft.
If my brother were girded with your power, and you
Were Claudio, you could have fallen like him,
Yet my brother would not be so severe."

XI

Her reproach
Confounded Angelo. His grim eyes flashing,
He softly said, "Please leave me."
But the modest girl became more bold and ardent

Minute by minute. "Just think," she said, "just think—
What if the One who by His righteous power
Forgives and heals were to judge us sinners
Mercilessly; tell me: what would become of us?
Think—and you'll hear the voice of love in your heart,
And your lips will breathe tender mercy,
And you will become a new man."

XII

He replied:
"Away, your pleading is a waste of time.
It is the law that punishes, not I.
I cannot save your brother. He will die
Tomorrow."

ISABELLA

What? Tomorrow? No, no,
He's not prepared yet, he can't be executed . . .
We will not so imprudently send our Lord
This hasty sacrifice. Even chickens are not killed
Before their time. Don't execute so quickly.
Save him, save him: in fact, my lord, you know
The poor youth has been condemned for a crime
That up to now was forgiven everyone.
He'll be the first one to be punished for it.

ANGELO

The law wasn't dead, it was simply slumbering.
Now it's awake.

ISABELLA

Be merciful!

ANGELO

I can't be.

To cover up a sin is the same crime.
By punishing one, I will be saving many.

ISABELLA

Aren't you the first to pronounce this terrible sentence?
And the first victim will be my unlucky brother.
No, no! Be merciful! Can it be your soul
Is without guilt? Ask it: can it be
No sinful thought has ever smoldered in it?

XIII

He shuddered involuntarily, hung his head,
And was about to leave. She: "Wait, wait!
Listen, come back. I'll shower you with great gifts . . .
Accept these gifts from me. They are not earthly,
But honorable and good. You would do well
To share them with heaven: I'll give you my soul's prayer
Before the break of day, in midnight silence,
Prayers of love, humility, and peace,
Prayers of the holy virgins, beloved of heaven,
Who have already died to the world in solitude,
But live for the Lord."
                          Abashed and subdued,
He arranged to meet with her the following day
And hurried off to his own private quarters.

PART TWO

I

For the whole day Angelo, speechless and sullen,
Sat alone, immersed in a single thought,
A single desire; all night sleep did not touch
His weary eyes. "What is it?" he kept thinking.
"Can it be I love her, since I want so much
To hear her again and let my eyes enjoy
Her maidenly charm? My soul sweetly
Pines for her . . . or is it that when the devil
Wants to catch a saint he arms his hook
With a saintly lure? Never in my life
Have I been tempted by immodest beauty,
And I am vanquished now by a pure virgin.
To me a man in love had always seemed
Ridiculous, and I wondered at his madness.
But now! . . ."

II

He wanted to reflect, to pray,
But reflection and prayer were distracted. In his words
He spoke to heaven, but his will and dreams
Longed for her alone. Sunk in dejection,
He chewed the name of God with an idle mouth,
But sin seethed in his heart. Inner anxiety
Overwhelmed him. Governing became unbearable,
Like a practical book, long known by heart.
He was bored; he was ready to renounce
His rank like a heavy yoke; and his sagacious
Dignity, of which he was so proud,
And which the folk admired so senselessly,
He valued as nothing and compared to a feather
Blown into the air by a gust of wind . . .

In the morning Isabella came to Angelo
And had a strange conversation with the governor.

III

ANGELO

Well, what is it?

ISABELLA

I want to learn your will.

ANGELO

Ah, if only you could guess it! . . . No, your brother
Must not live . . . and yet he might.

ISABELLA

Then why
Can he not be forgiven?

ANGELO

Forgiven? What in the world
Is worse than this vile sin? Murder is less.

ISABELLA

Yes,
That's heaven's judgment, but are we not on earth?

ANGELO

That's how you think? Then here's a suggestion for you:
What if it was given you to decide
To leave your brother to the headsman's block
Or redeem him by sacrificing yourself
And surrendering your flesh to sin?

ISABELLA

I would sooner
Sacrifice my flesh than my soul.

ANGELO

I am not talking
About your soul now . . . The thing is this:
Your brother is condemned; is it not merciful
To save him by sin?

ISABELLA

I am ready to answer
Before God for my soul: there is no sin
In that, believe me. Save my brother!
That is mercy, not sin.

ANGELO

Will you want to save him,
If mercy weighs as much as sin in the scale?

ISABELLA

O, let my brother's salvation be my sin!
(If it is a sin at all.) For that I'm ready
To pray night and day.

ANGELO

No, listen to me.
Either you don't understand my words at all,
Or else you avoid understanding me on purpose.
I'll put it simply: your brother is condemned.

ISABELLA

Yes.

ANGELO

The law has sentenced him to death.

ISABELLA

It has.

ANGELO

There is one means of saving him.
(All this is tending toward a supposition,
And is merely a question and nothing more.)

Suppose the one man who alone could save him
(A friend of the judge, or an authority himself,
Able to interpret the law, to soften its awful meaning),
Was burning with a criminal desire for you
And asked that you redeem your brother's life
By your own fall—or else the law decides.
What do you say? How would your mind decide?

ISABELLA

For my brother, for myself, believe me, I would sooner
Resolve to wear the scars of whipping like rubies
And lie peacefully in the bloody coffin as in a bed,
Than defile myself.

ANGELO

Your brother will die.

ISABELLA

                              What of it?
He would, of course, choose the better path himself.
He would not dishonor his sister to save his soul.
Better my brother die once than I perish forever.

ANGELO

Why, then, did the decision of the court
Seem inhuman to you? You accused us
Of being hard-hearted. Was that so long ago?
Just now you called the righteous law tyrannical
And almost made a joke of your brother's sin.

ISABELLA

Forgive me, forgive me. In my heart I was
Involuntarily dissembling then. Alas!

I contradicted myself, trying to save
What's dear to me, and pretending to forgive
What I hate. We are weak.

ANGELO
                    I'm heartened by your confession.
So women are weak, I am convinced of that,
And I say to you: be a woman, and not more—
Or you'll be nothing. So obey the will
Of your destiny.

ISABELLA
                    I cannot understand you.

ANGELO
You will: I love you.

ISABELLA
                    Alas! What can I say?
My wretched brother loved his Julietta,
And he will die.

ANGELO
                    Love me and he will live.

ISABELLA
I know: having the authority to test others,
You would like to . . .

ANGELO
                    No, I swear to you
I will not go back on my word now, I swear it
On my honor.

ISABELLA

Oh, so much, so much honor!
And a matter of honor! . . . Deceiver! Demon of guile!
Sign Claudio's release for me at once,
Or our act and the blackness of your soul
I'll publish everywhere—and enough of your playing
The hypocrite before people.

ANGELO

Who will believe you?
I am known to the whole world for my strictness;
General opinion, my rank, my entire life,
And the very sentence on your brother's head
Will make your denunciation look like crazy slander.
I have just given free rein to my passion.
Think now and give yourself up to my will;
Drop this foolishness: the tears, the entreaties,
And the timid blushing. They won't save your brother
From death and suffering. Only by your submission
Can you redeem him from the fatal block.
I'll wait until tomorrow for your answer.
And know that I have no fear of your informing.
Say whatever you like, I will not waver.
All your truth won't overthrow my lie.

IV

He spoke and left. The innocent girl stood there
In horror. Raising her clear, beseeching eyes
And pure right hand to heaven,

She left the loathsome palace and hurried off
To the prison. The door opened, and her brother
Appeared before her.

V

                    In chains, in deep dejection,
Trying not to regret all worldly joys,
Still hoping to live, preparing himself to die,
He sat in silence, and there in a broad cloak,
Under a black cowl, a crucifix in his hand,
Bent with age, a monk was speaking.
The old man tried to prove to the young sufferer
That death and life are equal to each other,
That there is one immortal soul both here and there,
And that the sublunar world isn't worth a cent.
Poor Claudio sorrowfully agreed with him,
But his heart was taken with dear Julietta.
The young nun entered: "Peace be with you!" He turned,
Looked at his sister, and instantly revived.
"My Father," Isabella said to the monk,
"I would like to speak with my brother alone."
The monk left them.

VI

CLAUDIO
                    Well, dear sister,
What is it?

ISABELLA

Dear brother, your time has come.

CLAUDIO

So there's no salvation?

ISABELLA

No, unless I pay
For your head with my soul.

CLAUDIO

So there is a way?

ISABELLA

There is. You may live. The judge is ready to soften.
His mercy is demonic: it grants you life
In exchange for eternal suffering.

CLAUDIO

What?
Eternal prison?

ISABELLA

Prison without bars,
Without chains.

CLAUDIO

Explain, what is it?

ISABELLA

Dear heart,
Dear brother! I'm afraid . . . Listen, dear brother,
Are seven or eight years worth more to you
Than everlasting honor? Are you afraid to die?
What is death? A moment. And is there so much suffering?

A crushed worm suffers just as much in death
As a giant does.

CLAUDIO

Sister! Am I a coward?
Do I not have strength enough to go to my death?
Believe me, I'll renounce the world without a tremor,
If I must die, and meet the grave's dark night
Like a sweet maiden.

ISABELLA

That's my brother!
I know him; I hear our father's voice from the grave.
It's true: you must die; so then die sinlessly.
Listen, I won't hide anything from you:
That terrible judge, that cruel hypocrite,
Whose stern gaze fills everyone with fear,
Whose lofty speech sends young men to the block,
Is a demon; his heart is black as deepest hell
And filled with vileness.

CLAUDIO

The governor?

ISABELLA

Hell clothed him

In its own armor. A deceitful man! . . .
I tell you: if I agreed to satisfy
His shameful desires, then you could live.

CLAUDIO

Oh, no, you mustn't.

ISABELLA

He said
I must hasten to the vile tryst this very night,
Or you will die tomorrow.

CLAUDIO

Don't go, sister.

ISABELLA

Dear brother! God is my witness:
If with my death alone I could save you
From execution, I'd value my life no more
Than a little pin.

CLAUDIO

Bless you, my dear friend!

ISABELLA

So tomorrow, Claudio, be ready for death.

CLAUDIO

Yes, so . . . passions seethe in him so strongly!
It's not a sin; or of the seven sins
This is the least?

ISABELLA

How do you mean?

CLAUDIO

It must be
They do not punish this transgression there.
Would he choose his own eternal ruin
For the sake of one moment? No, I don't think so.
He's intelligent. Ah, Isabella!

ISABELLA
What? What is it?

CLAUDIO
Death is terrible!

ISABELLA
So is shame.

CLAUDIO
Yes—
And yet . . . To die, to go into the unknown, to rot
In a cold, cramped coffin . . . Alas! The earth is beautiful
And life is sweet. But to go into dumb darkness,
To be thrown headlong into boiling pitch,
Or freeze in a block of ice, or race
Through endless emptiness borne by a swift wind . . .
And all that a despairing mind imagines . . .
No, no: life on earth in sickness, in poverty,
In sorrow, old age, prison . . . would be paradise
Compared to all we foresee after death.

ISABELLA
O God!

CLAUDIO
Sister! My friend! Let me live.
If it is a sin to save a brother from death,
Nature will forgive you.

ISABELLA
You dare to say that!
Coward! Soulless creature! You want life
At the cost of your own sister's depravity . . .

Incestuous! No, I can't think it was my father
Who gave you life and light. God forgive me!
No, my mother must have defiled my father's bed
To bear you! Die! If I could save you
By my will alone, you'd still be executed.
I have a thousand prayers for your death,
And not one for your life . . .

CLAUDIO
                    Sister, sister, wait!
Forgive me, sister!

VII

                    And the young prisoner
Clutched her dress to hold her back. Isabella
Overcame her anger with difficulty,
And forgave her poor brother, and again,
Tenderly, began to comfort the sufferer.

PART THREE

I

Meanwhile the monk stood by the open door
And heard the conversation between brother and sister.
It is time I told you that this old monk
Was none other than the Duke himself in disguise.
While the people thought he was in foreign lands
And called him, jokingly, a wandering comet,
He hid in the crowd, saw everything, observed
And invisibly eavesdropped, visiting
Palaces, squares, monasteries, hospices,
Bawdy houses, theaters, prisons. Endowed
With a lively imagination, the duke liked novels,
And perhaps wanted to imitate the caliph
Harun al-Rashid. Having overheard the story
Of the young recluse, he was deeply moved
And made up his mind at once, not only to punish
Cruelty and offense, but to set something right . . .
He quietly went in, called to the girl,
And took her to a corner. "I heard everything,"
He said. "You are worthy of praise;
You fulfilled your duty sacredly; but now

Follow my advice. Be at peace,
All's for the better; obey and trust me."
Then he explained what he proposed to do,
Gave her his blessing, and took his leave.

II

Friends! will you believe that a gloomy brow,
The sad mirror of a sullen, evil soul,
Attached a woman's desires to itself forever
And was able to be pleasing to a gentle beauty?
A wonder, isn't it? But it's so. This haughty Angelo,
This wicked man, this sinner—
Was loved by a tender, sad, and humble soul,
A soul rejected by its tormentor. He had been
Long married. Light-winged rumor flew about,
And did not spare his young wife, sneeringly
Reproaching her without proof; and he
Drove her away, saying haughtily:
"Perhaps rumor's accusation is false,
It doesn't matter. Suspicion must not touch
Caesar's wife." After that she lived alone,
On the outskirts, languishing in sorrow. The Duke
Remembered her, and at the monk's advice
The young maiden went to visit her.

III

Mariana sat by the window spinning
And weeping softly. Like an angel, Isabella
Appeared unexpectedly at her door.
The recluse had long been acquainted with her
And often came to comfort the poor woman.
She explained the old monk's plan to her at once.
As soon as the dark of night fell, Mariana
Was to go to Angelo's palace, meet with him
By the stone wall in the garden,
And having granted him the agreed reward,
Was to whisper barely audibly as she left
Just one thing: *Now do not forget my brother.*
Poor Mariana, smiling through her tears,
Tremblingly prepared—and the maiden left her.

IV

All night in prison the Duke awaited the results
And, sitting with Claudio, tried to comfort him.
Before dawn Isabella came again.
Everything had gone well: now pale Mariana
Sat with them, having successfully returned
And deceived her husband. The new day broke—
Suddenly a messenger came with a sealed order
For the prison warden. They read it: What? The governor
Ordered that the prisoner be executed at once
And that his head be presented to the palace.

V

Conceiving a new plot, the Duke produced
His ring and seal for the prison warden and stopped
The execution, and to Angelo he sent
Another head, ordering it shaved and taken
From the broad shoulders of a pirate who had died
Of a fever in the prison that same night,
And he himself set out with the intention
Of exposing to the whole world the wicked courtier
Who committed his vile deeds in darkness.

VI

                                        No sooner
Had the vague rumor of Claudio's execution
Spread than other news arrived. It was learned
That the Duke himself was coming back to town.
Crowds of people rushed to meet him. And Angelo,
Confused, feeling pangs of conscience, oppressed
By some foreboding, also hurried there.
Smiling, the kind Duke greets the people
Who crowd around him and offers a friendly hand
To Angelo. Suddenly a cry rings out—and the maiden
Falls at the Duke's feet: "Be merciful, my lord!
You are the shield of the innocent, the altar of mercy,
Be merciful! . . ." Angelo turns pale and trembles
And fixes a wild gaze on Isabella . . .
But masters himself. Recovering in time,

"She's mad," he says, "seeing that her brother
Has been condemned to death. This loss
Has deprived her of reason . . ."
                              Now showing wrath
And the indignation long hidden in his soul,
"I know everything," the Duke said, "everything!
Villainy will finally be requited on earth.
Maiden, Angelo, follow me to the palace!"

VII

By the throne in the palace stood Mariana
And poor Claudio. The villain, seeing them,
Shuddered, hung his head, and remained silent;
Everything became clear, and the truth emerged
From the fog; the Duke then: "Tell me, Angelo,
What do you deserve?" Without tears, without fear,
With grim firmness he answered: "Execution.
And I ask for one thing: order that my death
Be carried out quickly."
                              "Go," said the ruler,
"May the mercenary judge and seducer perish."
But the poor wife, falling at his feet, said:
"Have mercy. You have given me back my husband.
Don't mock me, don't take him away again."
"It is not I, it is Angelo who mocked you,"
The Duke replied, "but I will tend to your fate
Myself. His property will remain with you,
And you'll be rewarded with a better husband."
"I need no better one. Have mercy, my lord!

Don't be implacable, your hand joined me with him!
Otherwise why was I so long a widow?
He only paid his dues to being human.
Sister! Save me, my dear friend! Isabella!
Entreat for him, go on your knees,
Or keep silent but raise your hand!"

                       Isabella,
Like an angel, pitied the sinner in her soul,
And going on her knees before the governor,
Said, "Have mercy, my lord. Do not condemn him
Because of me. As far as I know and think,
He lived both righteously and honestly
As long as he had not set his eyes on me.
Do forgive him!"

            And the Duke forgave him.

THE ADOLESCENT
by Fyodor Dostoevsky

The narrator and protagonist of Dostoevsky's novel *The Adolescent* (first published in English as *A Raw Youth*) is Arkady Dolgoruky, a naïve nineteen-year-old bursting with ambition and opinions. The illegitimate son of a dissipated landowner, Arkady is torn between a desire to expose his father's wrongdoing and a desire to win his love. He travels to Saint Petersburg to confront the father he barely knows, inspired by an inchoate dream of communion and armed with a mysterious document that he believes gives him power over others. This new English version by the most acclaimed of Dostoevsky's translators is a masterpiece of pathos and high comedy.

Fiction

DEMONS
by Fyodor Dostoevsky

Inspired by the true story of a political murder that horrified Russians in 1869, Dostoevsky conceived of *Demons* as a "novel-pamphlet" in which he would say everything about the plague of materialist ideology that he saw infecting his native land. What emerged was a prophetic and ferociously funny tale of ideology and murder in prerevolutionary Russia.

Fiction

THE IDIOT
by Fyodor Dostoevsky

After his great portrayal of a guilty man in *Crime and Punishment*, Dostoevsky set out in *The Idiot* to portray a man of pure innocence. Twenty-six-year-old Prince Myshkin, following a stay of several years in a Swiss sanatorium, returns to Russia to collect an inheritance and "be among people." Even before Myshkin reaches home, he meets the dark Rogozhin, a rich merchant's son whose obsession with the beautiful Nastasya Filippovna eventually draws all three characters into a tragic denouement. In Petersburg the prince finds himself a stranger in a society obsessed with money, power, and manipulation. Scandal escalates to murder as Dostoevsky traces the surprising effect of this "positively beautiful man" on the people around him, leading to a final scene that is one of the most powerful in all of world literature.

Fiction

VINTAGE CLASSICS
Available wherever books are sold.
vintagebooks.com